SILENT SCREAMS

Releasing the Pain of Life's Experiences Through the Healing Power of the Written Word

LJ CRAWFORD

Limits of Liability and Disclaimer of Warranty

The author and publisher shall not be liable for your misuse of this material. This book is strictly for informational and educational purposes.

Warning – Disclaimer

This is a work of fiction. Names, characters, business, places, events, and incidents are either the products of the author's imagination or used in a fictitious manner. Any resemblance to actual persons, living or dead or actual events is purely coincidental.

Collaborations:
Photographer- Unlimited Photography Wallace Jenkins
Editor- Shavonna Bush
Cover Model-Jasmine J Moss

LJ Crawford
PO Box 1483
Hixson, TN 37343
LJCtheauthor@gmail.com
Ljcmotivations.com

Printed in the United States of America
First Printing, 2016
ISBN 978-1-941749-53-1
Library of Congress Catalog Number 2016911382
4-P Publishing
Chattanooga, TN 3741

THE FREEDOM IN MY PEN

I write to free myself of words and questions that are locked down in my mind and soul

I write to tell the world what I feel be it good or bad

I write to express thoughts of love, joy, loneliness, anticipation and longing

I write to say words that may make me cry or lose a grip on what I would like to say verbally

I write to share thoughts of love and contentment to a loved one

During this period in my life, I write to keep my inner being healthy and alert

But mainly I write to keep my sanity

LJ Crawford

ACKNOWLEDGEMENTS

I want to thank God for blessing me with a heart and mind to write a book of this nature to help others feel that they are not alone. A special thanks to my family for understanding the time restraints needed to produce this project. That alone has been a priceless experience. To know the heart of a writer requires that you respect the need for them to stay focused.

Thank you to the SWAT family of authors, mentors, and the highly esteemed Coach Laura Brown. Thank you, Donna Marie, for hanging in there with me as we sat at Panera Bread for four hours every night crying, laughing and critiquing each other's work.

Special thanks to my loving supporter of technology and positive words. Every time I opened my laptop, my heart was filled with gratefulness. Thank you!

Finally, I want to thank life for taking me down the hard paths and through the turbulent depths of pain and heartache. In spite of it all, I am still here, still strong and determined to help others learn to love themselves; never to feel stuck in the silent screams of their past but to live the life that they have been designed to live.

ABOUT THE AUTHOR

 LJ. Crawford is the founder of LJC Motivations. The goal of the company is to assist businesses with their workplace cultures and communication between management and hourly employees. LJ would like to see the workplace be an environment of growth, development and reaching the budget requirements with eager and determined team members that feel as though they are a part of the vision. LJ has a divine calling to help individuals recognize their greatness and honor the gifts that they carry within. Inspiring others is the foundation for LJC Motivations. An inspired heart and mindset is the key to a well-balanced personal and business life.

She is a Certified Purpose Discovery Specialist and a Certified City Strategist.

Though life has been an uphill journey, LJ has garnered grace, mercy, and lessons of growth along the way.

LJ considers herself a servant to the suffering and her genuine love for others allows her to counsel and actively guide people to another level of life and the necessity of self-love.

A native of Chattanooga, Tennessee, she enjoys spending time with her family and gets temporarily lost in the smiles and eyes of her two grandchildren. Networking and connecting people are LJ's greatest skills and passions. Iron sharpens iron so staying connected to individuals with positive mindsets is the key to advancement. At the age of forty-six, LJ skydived from twelve thousand feet, and the greatest moment was realizing that once you are committed, there is no turning back.

FOREWORD

LJ illuminates any room with professionalism and personality! Her story of survival and perseverance is the epitome of triumph. I have the honor of calling LJ Crawford, my friend. I have witnessed her progressions through winning local speech competitions, to leading her hospitality division in sales, to becoming a self-published author.

Lisa walks the talk! She demonstrates and commands excellence. Whether as a team member or a team leader, she is the perfect balance of blending relationships while acquiring results.

Vincent Ivan Phipps, M.A., CSP (Certified Speaking Professional)

Owner of Communication VIP Training and Coaching

Author of Speak Like a Pro!

CONTENTS

INTRODUCTION

Silent Screams was brought to life by my experiences and the soul disturbing silence from within the depths of me. Some of the chapters are graphic due to the weight of emotion that saturated me during the time of writing this book. The life of each character projects the deep need of a person to find their truth, understand their worth and the inability to deal with the silence of their life's devastating blows.

You may never tell a soul what has happened to you in your life or the feelings that suffocate you when you are alone; this is my plea to you, do not hold it inside. If you cannot tell anyone, the pad and pen will save you from depression, sadness and feeling as if no one understands. There is power in the written word.

Once you feel whole within but you still don't want to share your experiences, and you don't want to write a book or give a speech; go to a safe place, and have yourself a little fire with those pages. Watch the ashes as they fly away and find themselves as far away from you as possible. There is peace in that feeling.

THE SECRET OF THE INVISIBLE CHILD

When You Look Into My Eyes,
Do You Really See Me?

To feel genuine love was all Emeline wanted as a child. To her family, she was loved unconditionally, but to this 8-year-old she was alone.

"Emeline, come on, let's go!"

"Where are we going, momma?"

"We are going to your grandmothers."

Emeline did not like her grandmother's house because it was too hot and smelled funny.

"Momma, do I have to stay over there or am I coming back home with you?"

Her mom, Shirley Percy was a woman about town. Therefore, she was often left at her grandmother's house.

She said, "Girl, let's go!"

"But momma I need to know."

"Quit talking Emeline and get in the car.

No discussion meant, "Yes, kid you are staying."

I noticed how momma was in my room. The drawers were opening and closing, so, I knew that a bag was being packed. Ugh! At eight years old, I dreaded the trip to grandma's house. I thought that being with grandma was supposed to be fun and exciting, however, it was as if my world stopped and sadness and loneliness took over my entire being. Who could I tell that that house made me sick and who would care?

Finally, momma said, "We will make a couple of stops before we get to grandma's house."

This news perked me up and made me smile. The later I got there the better.

Momma took me to the store and bought me a new doll, some crayons, and a coloring book. Then, we went to get a big fat hamburger from this place called Georgia's. They had a jukebox and big creamy milkshakes with a cherry on top. We laughed and talked about my little play group and my teacher. My teacher was super nice even when she had to be fussy; I still liked her so much. When the other kids were playing at recess, she would pull me aside and teach me how to spell new words and read things about the archeologist and things in the earth. Ms. Trexler told me that when you learn to read really well, you could get lost in a book, leave your surroundings, and go somewhere new and adventurous. I loved that idea. I asked for books all the time that were harder than what I could read so that I could get lost in the words.

"Are you full?" Momma asked.

"Yes, ma'am."

She kissed my forehead, wiped my face and said, "Let's go."

We had the windows down, the music up and it was a great ride. Just the two of us and I was happy.

When we turned down my grandma's street, my happiness went out of the window just as fast as the cool breeze was coming in. She pulled into the dreaded driveway, and I just sat there as if she were going to run in and come back out and we were going home.

However, she said, "Emeline, get out! Let's go!"

Slowly I got out of the car and grabbed my toys and my overnight bag.

"Momma, what time will you be back to get me?"

"I will be back in the morning."

I looked up at her and quietly repeated in my head, "do not leave me here, please," but she did not hear me or feel my resistance.

Seeing that this was going to happen no matter what, I stopped on the front porch while she went inside to greet her mother. It was nice and peaceful on the porch; it was my place of happiness in the quiet house of hell. After about thirty minutes, momma came out, kissed me on the top of my head and said, "See you in the morning baby girl."

I walked her to the car and looked deeply into her eyes screaming in my head "do not leave me here," but she did not hear me.

As she backed out of the driveway, I prepared myself for the night ahead. I never knew if I was going to have a good night or a scary night at this house of confusion.

Grandma called out, "Emeline are you hungry?"

"No Ma'am we just ate."

"Okay!"

I sat on the porch and played with my doll until I got thirsty.

"Grandma, may I have something to drink?"

"Sure, I made some lemonade."

That was exciting because her lemonade was a perfect mix of sweet and tart. She asked to see my doll and helped me put on her a new outfit. It was nice. We watched a cowboy movie and ate cookies until she said it was time to get ready for bed. It was a good night because it was just us and I was visible to her, for tonight anyway. I took a bubble bath and washed my dolls hair. My grandma sat right there, laughed and played with me. It was a great night. I went to bed and was excited to be awakened by the sun because it meant I would see my mom soon. I called her very early to see what time she was coming.

She asked, "Did you have fun?"

"Yes," I said.

"Well, I need to pick you up in the morning."

"Momma. I do not want to be here another full day. Come and get me!"

She said, "Love. I will see you in the morning. Promise." The line went dead.

My grandma said, "Come on, let's eat."

She had fixed a good breakfast, but I wasn't really hungry. I knew that at some point of the day, her mood would change and my life would become an emotional nightmare. After breakfast, she made me help her clean up and plant some flowers she had bought the day before; I rather liked the dirt so that part was not so bad. Then it happened, she started fussing at me for no reason and calling me names.

She said, "Hurry your fat self up and go get some water to put in the dirt. I told you to bring the water pitcher. You are so ignorant you do not listen to anything. God, I could just knock you clean out."

I ran to the side of the house to hide, but after a while, she found me and started hitting me with a hose. At this point, anything could happen. I learned to be quiet and sit very still until the next outburst.

One Saturday, the yardman came to cut the grass and trim the bushes. I hated to see him coming because he looked weird and smelled funny. I did not like being there on Saturdays when he came. At first, he was nice to me because I helped him with the yard work, and he would do funny things and made me laugh.

Grandma asked, "Do you like him?"

"He is okay." I answered.

She said, "Well, I am going to run some errands, and I will be back."

Everything went fine that day. My mom ended up coming while my grandma was gone and she spoke to the family friend, the yardman, and we left.

I had to realize that the weekends would be my mom's time to enjoy her life so I quit resisting going to grandma's house and took the emotional demolitions so that momma could be free before going back to work on Monday.

The third time grandma left me with the yardman, it started to rain, so he put up the lawn mower and said, "Come on, let's sit on the swing for a while until the rain stops."

He said, "Emeline sit on my lap and let's see how high we can get this swing to go."

That sounded logical to me because I loved to swing at school, but you could only go high if you were sitting just right on the swing. He wanted me to face him. I thought that was weird, but I did it anyway. Every time the swing moved up, he held me by my butt and pulled me into him. Then I started feeling something, and he was looking crazy in the face.

"I want to stop," I said.

He stopped the swing, and I sat in the chair. By that time, my grandma came up that dreaded driveway; the yardman jumped up and went in the house to the bathroom. What was that about, I wondered?

The next weekend when grandma left, he asked, "Do you want something to drink? It is so hot out here today."

He spilled a drink all over my shirt and shorts.

"Go in there and change before your granny comes back."

I took my bag and got out some more clothes, but when I turned around, he was standing right there.

"Turn around and let me help you."

"I can do it," I said.

He hit me on the butt and said, "don't sass me, girl."

I gave him my clothes, and he touched me all over and smiled. I cried, and he smiled again. By the time my grandma got home, we were back on the porch. She did not even notice my clothes were different so, I did not say a word.

When he was leaving, he asked my grandma if I would be back next week because I was a good little helper.

"She probably will. She needs to be out in the sun doing work. She is so fat, and her body is growing too fast."

He smiled at me and tears came to my eyes. I was afraid but didn't know why.

My momma came and picked me up that afternoon instead of Sunday morning. I was relieved. I went home, sat in my room and wondered why he asked about me coming next week. I tried to think of a way to tell my mom that I did not want to go to grandma's next weekend, but I could hear her on the phone saying, "Oh, I can help you next Friday night and Saturday morning with your Fathers retirement gathering." Ugh!

The week went by so fast, and for some reason, all I could think about is being sick so I wouldn't have to go to my grandma's. My mom kept me at home on Friday night, but my grandma called for me to spend the night to help the yardman plant some flowers.

When my mom said I was really going, I just felt sick in my heart. She dropped me off, and he came as soon as she pulled off. My grandma had bought a ton of flowers and gave specific instructions on how and where she wanted each plant type to be planted. Once she finished barring those orders, she left.

I tried to stay in the front yard so that the neighbor women could see me and I could see them. I did not want him hitting me or touching me today.

Sure enough, I hear, "Emeline, come around here and help me."

There was an old shed in the back of the house; he wanted me to help him find a digging spoon. The shed was old and stinky. It had all kinds of tools in it for the house and yard. As soon as I walked in, he shut the door, and it was dark, but I saw his face. He smelled like beer or something when he spoke to me.

"Emeline, go over in that corner and look for a hoe."

"What is that?"

He said, "It is you today!"

I did not know what he was talking about. He kept drinking out of a bottle and touching his pants in the front.

I said, "I can't see in here, open the door so I can find the hoe thing."

There was a tall table in the shed. He jerked me up, sat me up there, and started touching me in my no touch place.

"Don't do that!"

"Shut up, you little hoe."

Then he put his hand over my mouth, stuck his hard, dirty finger inside my shorts and then inside my panties. He just kept doing that and smiling at me while I silently cried and tried to breathe.

He moved his hand and said, "Don't say a word."

He unzipped his pants and started to touch himself in the front. I screamed, and he knocked me off the table to the ground. It was cold and hard, and a bug of some kind immediately crawled on me. He yanked my shorts and panties down and climbed on top of me. I felt something hard and big, pushing its way inside of me. I thought that I was dying. I was hurting so badly, and I could not breathe because he was moving his body in and out of me and putting all of his weight on me while his hand was over my mouth. He made a bunch of noise, then just fell on me and laid there.

I could feel something wet flowing down both sides of my legs and down my face. He was laughing and saying things that made no sense to me. "

"You are my little hoe, now. You will always be my sweet love thang every week."

When he moved off me, he just left the shed and didn't say a word. I tried to move but couldn't, so I just laid there and cried. Finally, I heard my grandma calling my name. I cried louder and screamed for her to come to me.

"Girl, what happened to your clothes? They have blood and dirt all over them."

I didn't have to tell her what happened because it was as if she knew. She told me to get up, and we went into the house.

She gave me a bath and told me that this happened to me because I was so fast.

"You got those big ole legs and little boobs, and carry on a conversation like you are a grown woman so he just got carried away thinking you were older. You will be okay. Emeline, don't tell your momma. I'll take care of him."

Even as a child, I knew that was wrong. She was extra kind to me that night. I could hardly walk the next morning.

When my momma came, she said, "Baby, what's wrong with you?"

My grandma said, "She just worked hard yesterday. That's all."

I got home, went to my room and just sat there holding my doll.

I stopped eating, playing and talking so much but no one, I mean no one noticed. My life had been changed from within, and I couldn't tell a soul.

THE SECRET LIFE OF HIGH SCHOOL

The Betrayal of a"Friend"Leads to a Life Without Trust

I struggle within myself to be an individual yet I struggle outside of myself to fit in with the crowd. On top of that struggle, I am a junior, coming to a new high school where I don't know a soul. Good grief! My dad is in the military, and we had to move to the south so that he could do some contract work for two years. My father is strong and tough but loving.

My mom died when I was fourteen. Therefore, a three-year-old wound is still trying to destroy me. Life moves forward, and I have to graduate so I can go to the college and stay in one place for four years.

My name is Larissa Jones. Today is the first day of my new school adventure and trust me; every new school is a journey of craziness for the new kid. I could hear my dad in the kitchen making my breakfast smoothie as he did every morning. My dad, Colonel Jacob Jones was extremely strict about the food he bought and what we ate. So needless to say no fast food. Man, what I wouldn't give for some McDonald's or a greasy hash brown. He would probably punish me for eating that stuff. It's cool though because I was a gymnast, runner, and super fit. This was an excellent way to feel about yourself at sixteen years old but then came a new high school with new girls and boys.

"Larissa, I am finished with breakfast. Do you want me to drive you? Are you okay with driving in alone?"

"Dad, as long as you have filled out all of the paperwork, then I will drive alone."

He said, "Come on in and let's talk for a second." I went into the kitchen.

"Remember you are a unique and beautiful young lady. Do not let the ways of this city and the mindsets of these kids stop you from being Larissa LJ Jones. Okay."

"Yes, daddy! Love you." I grabbed my keys and left.

This school was enormous with three floors. I found it odd that my daddy put me in a Liberal Arts School. I only dabbled in art and theater. I was a pure athlete, but that is the life of an army kid, so you learn to go with the flow of your parent's life.

When I finally reached the school, there were four parking lots, and that alone let me know that this school would have a ton of students. I saw a student and asked him where to park since I did not have one of the colored tags yet. He said to park in the visitor's section until I get the pass, which awesome because it was right by the front door.

Upon entering the building, several people spoke to me, and I thought that must be a part of the southern hospitality trait here in the south. I am very nervous but excited that I will be able to finish my last two years of high school in one place. Thank goodness, dad's contract is for three years in this city.

Okay, Larissa let's get this day started. I went into the office. They were actually waiting for me with a packet of information and my class schedule. That almost never happens in my gypsy world. I went down the hallway and found my accelerated English class. The teacher was so boring but thank goodness the lessons were things I had done last year at this preppy private school I attended. There, they made us do so much work above the grade expectation it was ridiculous. During that time, I complained, but today I was grateful.

A girl named Grace asked to see my schedule, and it was unbelievable that she had the exact classes as I did. All of them! A new friend on the first day, awesome! Grace and I had so much in common. Her momma died when she was eleven just like mine, but she ended up living with her aunt instead of her dad. Grace seemed to have everything going for her. I liked her way of thinking, she was always challenging herself to be better, and I really admired that about her.

First full day of school was a huge success, and it seems as though the school was only scary in size, not the people. Although the school did not offer any sports, I still ran every day, and I signed up for a gymnastics class that wasn't too far away from my house. Since the work at school was fairly simple, this gave me a great way to fill up my evenings. My dad did not believe in idle time; all time should be accounted for and productive.

Grace started to come over and hang out with me on the weekends. She met my father, and that was cool. He was happy that I made a genuine friend.

After a few months, Grace said, "LJ ask your dad if you could spend the night at my house. We know how protective he is about his baby girl."

When I asked him, he said, "I was wondering what took so long. Sure you can!"

I was astonished at his quick response but excited at the same time.

"Do you want to meet her aunt?" I asked.

He said, "Well, I just happened to be at the school when Grace was being picked up, and she had to run back in the school for something. I casually introduced myself to the woman in the car. I asked her not to say anything because I did not want you to think I was spying on you."

Laughing, I said, "Okay, daddy that makes me feel better knowing that you aren't the super spy I thought you were."

The next week after school on Friday, I went over to meet all of Grace's family. I did not know that Grace lived in the house with grown men even though they were her cousins. I don't think we talked about them. Anyway, one of them was really cute. I didn't realize that I liked tattooed guys but dang! This one cousin was the bomb.com. His name was Mathias, and he was beautiful! Unfortunately, he was twenty-five, and that would never fly with my daddy, so I just kept my thoughts to myself.

The weekend was awesome. Grace's aunt allowed us to have a small get together and her fine cousin Mathias stayed for it. Now I have tried so hard to stay pure and leave boys or men out of the picture. Besides I figured, what's the use since my daddy was private eye number one and he knew me and my every move. I just didn't worry about anything really. What I have come to learn is that you can protect your children from the real world and make them as dumb as a box of rocks. Every man will not be like my daddy and won't have my best interest at heart.

We had a great time at the party. The next day was Sunday, and it was time to go home. As I was getting in my car to leave, Mathias came out of the house and asked me, when would I be eighteen years old?

I said, "On June 5th, so about four months away."

"Why?" I asked.

He said, "I just wanted to know LJ."

"LJ? My name is Larissa."

"No, with me, you will be LJ, it's easier, and it will be my pet name for you."

I said, "Pet names are usually given if you like another person."

He replied, "Then that is my pet name for you. You just need to be older."

I just smiled and said, "See ya later, Mathias." I blushed all the way home.

Grace lived in a nice neighborhood. I noticed that when I was with her, I dressed differently and spoke differently. I knew this about myself, so it was easy for me to change back and forth between my school personality and my home personality.

I got home, and it was business as usual with my daddy. He did not notice a change in me. This is interesting; I thought dad would surely smell the fact that I was starting to like a twenty-five year old man.

Okay, here we go. My double life will begin today. From that weekend on it seemed like I was always over at Grace's house. Mathias was always there. He was fantastic to look at, and he wanted to be with me.

One weekend, Grace's auntie was not coming home until late because she had to work and was going straight on a trip with her boyfriend for the weekend after work.

Grace asked, "Do you want to come over? My aunt will be gone, and we can have a little party or something."

"That sounds great." I said.

By being Grace's friend, I became very popular at school. It was really cool to be a part of the in crowd. I wasn't used to this much attention at the other schools that I attended. So, this was fun. However, on this unchaperoned weekend, things went sideways.

It was the beginning of real secrets of LJ. That Friday night we all sat around watching movies, eating pizza, laughing and talking. Nothing out of the norm until my sweet Grace said, "Larissa, I am going to go out for a little while with my boyfriend."

"What about me?" I said.

"Stay here and watch a movie with Matthias. He likes you anyway. You will be all right."

My first thought was my daddy would lose his mind if he knew I was in the house with this grown man without any supervision. What to do?

Grace left, and Mathias said, "LJ come sit by me, girl. I am not going to bite you unless you want me to."

I totally did not know what that meant. Instead of asking, I just went over and sat by him. He smelled good. Gee whiz; I am not sure I have ever felt this way before in my life. What I did know is that this would piss my dad off if he knew. I talked myself into staying to watch a movie and then I thought it would be best if I went home and kept myself from doing or saying anything stupid or more than anything lying to my daddy about my weekend.

We watched "Fast and Furious 7," I love Dewayne the Rock Johnson. He is Samoan like my dear friend from Hawaii, Talaleu Matautia. She was Samoan and a princess. She was the best friend I'd ever had in my life. We were sisters in spirit. We lived in Hawaii for eight years of my life, and I met her as soon as I got there. It was a great friendship. She is the sister I never had. I miss her so much. We talk at least once a week.

Anyway, Mathias kept trying to kiss me and touch me, so I said, "I need to go home and get something. I will come back after Grace comes home."

"You are not going anywhere," he said to me.

"Why?" I asked and started to get up.

"No, you have been flirting with me, and you know you want this."

I immediately thought, I never said a word to him. I simply admired him from within. So, I sat back down on the couch and did not move because I saw something like this on Lifetime. I thought nothing would happen to me. I sat quietly, wondering where my keys were just in case something weird happened.

He said, "Go on girl, I am just playing with you."

Oh my goodness, I was relieved. I got up and as I was going upstairs to get my bag and my keys Grace came home and said, "How about another movie?"

"Are you going to leave again?" I asked.

She said, "No girl, it's all good."

So, we watched another movie, but I couldn't stop thinking about how serious Mathias looked at me before he said he was just playing.

Grace and I called it a night around 2am. We woke up to the smell of biscuits, bacon, and coffee. I thought Grace's aunt had come back home, but as we walked down stairs, I heard Lil Wayne playing through the speakers. It was Mathias!

"What in the world is wrong with you boy; you never cook for this house." Grace said.

She poured us some coffee. We ate, cleaned up and got dressed to meet some of the girls from school at the mall so that we could get some outfits for tonight's little gathering.

I was excited. This would be my first house party. I made Grace promise not to leave me alone like she did last night.

She said, "No problem girl" and then she looked at me and asked, "Larissa are you a virgin?"

"Yes, like why wouldn't I be one?"

She just smirked and gave me a quick friend hug.

She said, "For your information, you are the only one that I know. I'm proud of you."

I told her I wanted to wait until I got married. That actually made her laugh.

I think that it is possible because it is my body, and no one has a right to it but me. I did notice that the clothes I chose were a little less revealing than the other girls' outfits, but I did not care. I bought it anyway, and I looked cute. My dad would have approved, so that was good enough for me.

By the time we got back to the house, we had cleaned up, ordered some pizzas, put out the chips and all of the party snacks. People started to pour into the house at 9pm. I thought that it was going to be about twenty people, but it looked like at least fifty came at one time. I was nervous about this. How will her aunt respond if she found out? I mentioned it to Grace. She told me to loosen up a little, so I did not bring it up again.

Some nice songs were playing. We even did a Kid and Play line and it was so cute and funny. It was hot in the house so I went outside to get some air. All of the sudden Mathias showed up and grabbed me from behind.

"Stop, what are you doing?" I asked.

"I am just playing with you girl." but he did not let me go.

His Aunt had an old Cadillac in the back yard, which was a good piece away from the house.

"Come on and walk with me," he said.

I was thinking it would be better walking than just standing still with this boy/man, so I agreed to walk.

We stopped at the car. "I'm going to sit down for a minute," he said.

I giggled, "I know you are not tired from a ten-minute walk"

He looked at me and all of the sudden he slapped me across the face and said, "What's funny Ms. Goody two shoes bitch?"

I was so stunned that he hit me; I was just trying to keep my balance in my heels in the soft grassy area. I started to walk away to go back to the house but Mathias grabbed me by the back of the hair and began dragging me back to the car. He shoved me into the backseat of the car. I tried so hard to fight him, but I was too small. His temperament kept changing between sweet and hateful.

I said, "I need to go Mathias." He acted like he did not hear me.

He said, "I heard you were a virgin. Well, that is going to change tonight because I'm going to be your first and this memory will stay with you forever."

"No, Mathias please don't do this to me!" I screamed.

I was naive, but I knew what rape was and that I did not want that to happen to me at all. I was already in the back seat of the car, but he let me sit up and started talking to me as if he wanted to be my boyfriend or something. I had an opportunity to go out of the other door, I pulled the lever but the door handle was broken and would not open. That just pissed him completely off. He grabbed me again, punched me in the stomach, pushed me back on the seat, and pulled my legs apart. I was screaming my heart out, but all I could hear was the music from the house.

"Scream all you want no one can hear you LJ."

My heart dropped from the pain and knowing that no one could save me from this psychotic man. Mathis tied my hands up over my head and then tied them to the door handle so that I could not move. He ripped my clothes off, and I lay there completely naked and humiliated.

He touched every part of my body. He put his hand around my throat and started to choke me and then it happened. I felt him inside of me. I was gasping for air and still trying to scream.

"Scream one more time, and you are going to be so sorry."

He took a knife from the back window and put it up to my throat.

"Should I make an example out of you for being such a goody two shoes?"

He moved his hand so that I could answer him.

I cried, "Please Mathias, I will be quiet. Come on honey just make love to me."

That seemed to calm him down. "Do you mean it LJ? Do you want me?"

"Yes, I do. Just don't hurt me, okay? I will be good and do what you want." I whimpered.

He lay on my naked body and started to rub me all over, acting as if he was going to sleep or something. I couldn't move my hands, so I took my legs and wrapped them around his waist so tight to see what was happening because he was not answering me or anything. When I squeezed him with my thighs, he thought I was trying to hurt him, so he slapped me again and rammed himself inside of me over and over again. I became numb inside of my pain; he wanted me to participate with him, like move my body or try to touch his back and scratch it.

I can't do any of that, my hands are tied up. Matthias, I will do it, but I need you to let me put my hands down so that I can hold you."

He cut the ropes off but kept his hand around my throat until I almost passed out. He was still inside of me screaming for me to rub his back and moan as if I liked it. I tried so hard to do what I was told, but I was in so much pain I could barely hear his demands. He finally reached his release or whatever it's called and said, "Now get dressed. You had better not tell a soul, or next time it will be worse on you. Do you hear me LJ?"

This fool brought baby wipes for me to wipe off which means that he planned this out. How and why do you plan to rape a girl that you knew wanted to be a virgin? Why would you do that? I was thinking to myself, as I got dressed.

"Look in that mirror and fix your face."

I am a fair-skinned girl, so my face looked a beat-up mess. My legs were bruised so badly it looked like I was in a car wreck.

I made it back to the house and found my way to Grace's room without being detected. I locked myself in her closet. I did not know what to do to myself so that no one would know what happened to me. So, I just sat there in the closet until I heard the music stop. I heard Grace asking Matthias if he had seen me anywhere. She said she had been looking for me everywhere.

"I don't know where that little goody, goody is." He snapped.

I sat there crying in silence as blood trickled down my legs. I tried to wipe it up. I was devastated that someone I thought I could trust would do this to me. My daddy told me all the time, everything that looked good was not good. I truly understand the meaning of this now. I understand in such a way that my life will never be the same.

I heard Grace in the room. She sat on the bed and was talking out loud to herself.

"Her purse and keys are here where could she be?"

I did not have a choice but to call her name.

"Larissa? Where are you?

"I'm in the closet. Wait! Go get a warm rag and put soap on it before you come in here."

Grace ran out of the room, and when she came back, I heard the bedroom door lock. I wasn't sure if it was her or Mathias.

The closet doorknob turned. I whispered, "Grace, is that you?

"Yes, let go of the door and let me in." I opened the door, and she closed it behind her.

She saw my face and body and asked, "What the hell happened to you, Larissa?"

"I was raped, Grace." I began to sob into her neck.

"Who did this to you?

"I can't tell you, Gracie, I can't tell.

Grace whispered to me and asked if it was Mathias.

"No it was not." I said immediately. She just looked at me as if she knew I was lying.

Her first thoughts went to my dad.

"Goodness, you have one day to heal, and then you have to go home. Your daddy is going to see this! What are we going to do?"

For a moment, it felt like she was more concerned about getting in trouble than about me.

"Let me help you take a bath with some Epsom salts to help with the pain. What are we going to do?"

I didn't hear anything, so I assumed that the party was over. I heard Mathias down stairs laughing with a girl. This nasty ass man had raped me and is trying to lay with someone else just like that? I was just a conquest to him. He is a man that took my innocence, violated my body, mind, and spirit.

After Grace had run the bath water, she helped me walk into the bathroom because I could barely move. It took all I had to walk up to the house from my place of loss, that big brown Cadillac in the yard with the broken door and the knife in the window. I thought of the soft grass that my heels sank into as I walked with a friend that turned to my most hated enemy.

Grace actually picked me up and laid me in the tub. "Larissa, my aunt has some muscle relaxers in her room. Please,let me give you one. It will help you rest, and your body will feel so much better during the night."

"Grace, the only way I could take that is if you promised not to leave me alone for one minute while I sleep." She promised that she wouldn't.

If she had truly been listening, she would have heard me telling her that Mathias raped me. But she was not.

Grace was a great friend. She washed all the blood off my legs, and she cleaned the gash that was in the back of my head. That explained the blood on my neck, chest, and shoulders. She made sure that there was nothing left for others to see but the marks around my wrists and some bruises on my legs. I jogged so much, so I was constantly in running gear, no one would be able to see anything. I also had a handprint across my cheek and a bruise on my stomach from his mighty punch. By the time the bath was over, I was so sleepy that Grace helped me slip on a pair of sweatpants and a hoodie. I was so cold and empty on the inside.

The next morning, I tried to get up and slip into the bathroom because I did not want to run into Mathias. As I was standing by the door to open it gently, I heard Grace ask Mathias, "Why did you have to beat her up so badly? I promised you that I would get her for you. Had I known you were going to do her like that I would have never done that! She is a good person."

What the hell was I hearing? I went back to bed and just lay there in utter disbelief and emptiness. My strength came to me, and I jumped up and packed my clothes. I put Grace's stuff on her bed and grabbed my keys and headed down the stairs like nothing was hurting me.

"See you guys later."

Grace jumped up, "Larissa I thought you were going to stay until Sunday night?"

"No, I need to get home."

Mathias looked at me like he was going to kill me because he did not know if I was going to the police or home. Grace was freaking out.

"Larissa, let me ride with you to your house."

"That's okay; I'm not feeling well. I am going home to lay down for a while in my bed, and maybe my dad will be home so we could talk."

"LJ, let me walk you to your car." Mathais interjected.

"Look, girl, I was drunk last night, and I don't know what happened to me, but I really do like you and want to be with you. Since I am your first, now, we have a special bond.

I do not know what clicked in my mind, but I said, "We have a bond, alright! You are going to need one, soon!"

"Don't play with me," he said angrily. Girl, if you tell someone, I will come into your house, take that knife and slit your throat. Do you want that? Then I will go in the next room and kill your precious daddy. Play with me on this LJ and see what happens to you both."

My weakness returned when he said that he would kill my dad. "Fine Mathias, you win!" He smirked and went into the house.

Thank goodness my dad was not at home when I got there. He left a note reminding me that he was out of town for the next two days. What a blessing! I had time to let these bruises heal and for me to feel better.

In one year, I moved to a great city and went to a great school. Met one of the sweetest girls that I have met since I left Hawaii. I was excited about the academics and the thought of staying at one school until I graduated.

In one weekend, I was violated physically, emotionally and spiritually by a man that took the one thing that I had total control over for his own personal use without my permission. I lost a friend that I felt so close to that we could have been sisters. She set me up to be destroyed by her cousin, Mathias. Betrayal, rape, threats of death all in one twenty-four hour period. My entire life has changed, and I can't tell a soul.

It was Sunday, and I was tired of thinking about everything. I couldn't stay out of school on Monday because my daddy does not play those games at all. My neighbor noticed my car at home and came over.

Joanne, she was a sweet lady that wanted to date my dad, but he was not having it right now. I did not understand him because he was a good-looking man and my mom has been dead for six years so if he thought I would have a problem with him dating, he is wrong.

I really need someone to take all of his focus off me because I can tell things are going to be changed with me.

Joanne knocked on the door and told me that my dad asked her to watch the house because I would not be back until late Sunday. She wanted to know if I was okay since it was just 9am in the morning and I was already at home. I told her I just needed to do some studying, so I cut my girls' weekend short. She asked if I had eaten. I thought about it, and I hadn't eaten in almost two days.

"I could eat a bite.

"Cool, you can come over and eat with us or pack it up and bring it back home."

I opted to just go there and hang for a minute with her kids.

She said her brother, Jonas, was there from Georgia.

As we were walking across the yard, Joanne asked, "Why are you limping?"

"I think that I pulled something in gymnastics class the other day."

"I know about that pain," she replied. She was once an athlete also.

Joanne had fixed so much food and I wanted some of everything. I hung out with them for a while, ate and laughed. Her brother was really funny and pretty like a girl. He was far from being a girl, though. He said that he had four kids and two ex-wives. No girl in that! I stayed with them for a few hours, we watched a movie, and I played with Joanne's kids. It was nice to be in a family setting. I missed my mom.

When I got home, I called my dad to check on him and to see if he had eaten anything.

He is so cool; he said, "I'm the dad, I am supposed to be asking you the questions. But, no, I have not eaten but since my seventeen year old mommy has called, I guess I better stop and eat."

He asked about how the weekend went at Grace's house. I said, it was okay.
I told him about me eating breakfast at Joanne's and meeting her brother and how good the food was.

"Daddy, why don't you take her out when you come home?"

"Here we go... Do you really think she is nice?" he asked?

"I do, daddy. She is awesome, and I believe that she is genuine.

"Well, we will see about it when I get back home."

I spent the next three months trying to heal my body without going to the doctor. Then it dawned on me that I had not had a period in two months. I knew it, but I tried to ignore it because I really did not know what I would do if I took a pregnancy test and that thing came back positive. I had not felt normal or like myself at all after the night of horror in the Cadillac.

I did not know who to confide in since my best friend was a liar and betrayal was the only thing I could feel when she came into my presence. I treated Grace no different because I did not know how to handle another female that would allow a man to rape another woman and know about it. My mind can't comprehend what kind of soul she possesses to do that to another person. In my book, she is worse than Mathias because she premeditated our friendship to set me up to be violated. I should probably speak to a therapist.

I began to get sicker and sicker as the months moved forward. My dad was out of town a lot during this time due to his work schedule, but I was able to stay at home so I could go to school. They were short trips, but they came at times when I was feeling my worse.

Gracie called me one Thursday night and asked me if I would like to go out with her family for dinner. She said, "Everyone misses you over here."

"I am not feeling well, so I will have to pass but thank you."

She said, "Mathias wants to see you. He thinks that you are hot."

"Really, like I said Grace, I am not feeling well. Talk to you soon."

What a joke, I thought. All of the sudden I felt a pain in my stomach that was so painful I thought I was going to die. I called, Joanne and asked her if she was busy.

"No sweetie, what do you need?"

I asked if she could come over and see me now. She must have run over because she was there before I could get the phone back on the hook. She came straight in and called my name. I was in the den doubled over. She asked me what was hurting. I told her my stomach was in excruciating pain, and I could barely breathe.

She said, "We are going to the hospital, we can drive, or we can call an ambulance. Which do you prefer? Just know that we are doing something right now! Choose Larissa!

"Car!" I yelled! Joanne sprinted next door and pulled the car in the driveway so I would not have to walk too far.

"How long have you been hurting like this, Larissa?"

"About three months," I whispered.

"What the hell girl? Anything could be wrong with you." Then she quickly apologized.

"It's okay. I'm stupid. I did not have anyone to talk to, and I couldn't talk to my daddy about this."

"Why not? Your dad will lasso the moon for you, and you know it.

"Joanne, I need to tell you something. You are as close to a momma that I can get. Don't be mad at me and please don't yell at me when I tell you."

"What is it honey, you can trust me."

"Joanne, I was raped at Grace's house a few months ago." I could see her grab the steering wheel so tight that her knuckles turned white.

"By whom?" she asked.

"I can't tell you because he said if I did, he would slit my throat and then kill my daddy. I just can't tell."

I told her every detail without giving her a name. She began to weep for me as if I were her child. We got to the emergency room, and I was hurting so bad. What in the world, had he done to me? They took me right on back because my blood pressure was so high. The nurse asked me a bunch of questions about sex, but I did not tell her that I was raped. I told her that I had been sexually active with one person.

"We are going to do some sexually transmitted disease tests on you as well; just to be sure you are okay."

The nurse was so nice. She stayed with me during the exam and held my hand during my first pap smear. It was embarrassing but comforting to have her there. The doctor stopped the exam and asked me if I had some type of trauma happen to me in the past few months.

I said, "No."

He said, "Call her mother in here."

"She is not my momma. She is my neighbor."

The doctor asked, "Do you trust her at all?"

"Yes, I do."

"Well, I need to bring her in here. Is that okay?"

I said, "Yes."

Joanne came in, took the place of the nurse, and held my hand.

The doctor said, "Larissa, were you raped? "I looked at Joanne, and she nodded for me to tell the truth.

"Yes."

"We are going to have to keep you overnight to inject some serious antibiotics into your system. We are going to have to make a report Larissa."

"No, I will not tell his name until I speak with my daddy."

"You can get dressed Larissa. Ms. Joanne, can you sign the paperwork for her to stay overnight since she is not of age?"

"I will," she said. "And I will stay with her tonight also."

This lady loved me, and I knew that I loved her too because she stroked my hair as if I were her own kid.

The doctor got the blood work back and had to do another pap smear and a vaginal ultrasound because he could not understand the amount of pain I was in. The ultrasound showed a little baby stuck in my fallopian tubes. Not only did I lose my virginity but I lost a baby also.

The doctor said, "It had damaged the tube, and he was going to have to remove it."

"Will I ever be able to have kids?!!"

"It's a possibility, but we have to look at what is going on right now, and this is the only way to stop the pain."

Broken and empty is how I felt at this moment. How can you recover from that feeling? You did nothing to deserve all of this, but someone took it upon himself to take your mind body and soul; abuse it just because they felt like it.

It took me months to heal and to get back to myself physically but mentally I turned into a demon possessed wounded female. I began living a double life; to the outside world, I was so sweet and loving. When it came to boys, men, thugs and married men, I wanted to get them to love me and then destroy them because in my mind I would get them before they got me. I would hurt them so bad that they would not hurt another woman ever again. This went on until I graduated from high school side by side with my *friend* of betrayal.

The night of the graduation, I knew that we were going to move, so I told Gracie what a rotten soul she had to set me up to be raped by her psycho cousin, Mathias. Who by the way is now in jail for going on a damn raping spree and got caught by this sweet girl's father. So I did not have to expose him for what he did to me, but my true pain was with Gracie.

She said, "Larissa! I am so sorry. How did you know that I had something to do with it?"

"I heard you and him speaking in the hallway the morning after the party."

She just cried, and I did not care at all until she said, "Mathias has been molesting me and raping me since I was a child. I just couldn't take it anymore. He said the only way I will stop is if you find me a small, fair-skinned, athletic girl and bring her to me. What was I supposed to do? I just knew that you would tell your dad and stop him, but you did not protect us."

Why in the hell was this flipped back on me? Then I wondered what would I have done in this situation if I were Gracie? I don't know, if someone is hurting you, the only objective is to get it to stop no matter what method or who you use. I looked at Gracie and wanted to punch her in the face and hug her at the same time. Ahhh! God help me!

She was crying so profusely on our graduation night that was supposed to be full of fun and figuring out which party we would attend first. Instead, we both have had to grow past the activities of new semi-adults to full-blown adult thoughts of forgiveness, love, healing and friendship. Gracie and I went to dinner with my parents. Oh yeah, I forgot to mention, during my year of promiscuity and self-destruction my dad and Joanne got married.

We welcomed, Gracie into our family because she had been ostracized by her family for testifying against Mathias. Really, what is wrong with people? They told her, what goes on in the house stays in the house. How many girls grow into destroyed women and suffer in silence because of this stupid ass saying?

THE SECRET MASK OF MARRIAGE

I Married Your Mask So Who Are You?

They say, 'the eyes are the windows to the soul.' However, I'm glad that I'm the only one looking. It's my wedding day. The full-length mirror shows a beautiful gown and veil, but when I look into my eyes, I know that I'm making a mistake. What am I doing?

"Lurleen, it's time!" I look to see my best friends standing behind me.

"I'm coming!" I yell back, playfully.

KJ said, "Good luck, girl! I'm right beside you."

I don't have a father, so I walked down the aisle alone, which was cool because Raj, my future husband, was singing to me. His voice was so melodic, and he sang with such passion, love, and dedication. He was singing "Always and Forever" because he constantly told me that no matter what, his love was real and would never fade. Red Flag! But did I pay attention? No!

The ceremony was beautiful. Raj and I met up in the hallway. He looked deeply into my eyes and asked, "What's wrong?"

"Nothing, I hope."

I had the strangest feeling about him at that moment; almost as if I didn't know him.

"Come, my wife. Let's party."

After the wedding, things changed. He quit calling me at work. He started staying out late. It happened so fast. I began wondering if all of the upfront love was just for show and now he could no longer keep up his act. Perhaps the feelings I had at the wedding were true.

My job was getting on my nerves, but I enjoyed having my own money and being independent, so when I was laid off, I was devastated. Two weeks later, I found out that I was six weeks pregnant. When I told Raj about the baby all he said was, "I hope it's a boy!"

As morning sickness set in and I wanted to die right there in the bathroom; he rolls over and rudely says, "Can you shut the door? I'm trying to sleep."

After being out all night, he smells of alcohol and cigarettes. Why does it have to be like this? Not to mention the fact that he gambled away the rent money. I don't know when I've ever cried so much. The feelings of rejection are overriding my happiness for being pregnant.

He tells me that he knows things aren't what they should be, but he's trying. How can he say he is trying when he hasn't bought groceries for two weeks, and the lights were cut off last month? I realize it is hard for him to be the only one working, but he makes significant money. We should be living in a house instead of a one-bedroom apartment.

I asked, "Why does Jason pick you up from work and then keep you out until three or four in the morning?"

"I have to work!"

"But Raj, your workday ends at 4pm. What's going on? You barely keep the lights on, and we got two late notices on the rent. I'm eight and a half months pregnant and all I've had today is a banana that the neighbor gave me. So what are you doing with the money because surely it isn't going to this house?"

Gathering his things, he screams, "Look! I am tired of arguing over money! I'm outta here!"

The sun rose and set for two days before I called my family to come and get me. Raj didn't call or anything. I went into labor the very day my family came to pack my things. My mom drove me to the hospital while my sister, Reann, and my brothers, Eric, Fred, and Willie, packed my belongings.

Someone in Raj's family must have seen me at the hospital because he came bursting through the curtain crying and begging for forgiveness. The look on my mom's face should have knocked him into another life.

She whispered in my ear, "Going back to him would be like eating your own puke!"

"Please forgive me. I don't know what happened. Please let me stay to see my child being born," he pleaded.

My heart melted with the tears he shed. My mom must have picked up on it because she left to call my family and friends.

"Honey, I'll be back in about twenty minutes," Raj promised before walking out of the door.

KJ was the first to arrive. I began to tell her about Raj. She said, "I want to tell you something, but I don't want to upset you."

"Go ahead," I said, "I don't think anything else can hurt more than this."

"Are you sure?"

"Go on, tell me!"

"Well, on my way in I saw Raj in his car kissing some girl."

"It couldn't be! He was just in here crying and begging for forgiveness!"

She said, "I wanted to be sure, so I called his name, and he looked at me and drove away."

I can't believe him. I was feeling sorry for his ass. I guess matters of the heart can hurt worse than these contractions.

"Whatever. Go get somebody because this baby is coming!"

I didn't think I could do it, but I delivered a baby girl. I named her Leala after Leala Ali, the boxer. I knew after all I'd gone through while carrying her she would be a fighter.

My room was filled with family and friends, but I was too tired to enjoy their company. When they left the nurse came in and took the baby back to the nursery. I was awake with thought and disbelief. How could Raj do this to me? I thought that we had some love in our relationship; that's why we got married. I heard the door open, and it was Raj and his mother.

His mother, Mrs. D, brought a huge basket of stuff for the baby.

Raj asked, "What did you name her?"

"Leala."

"I thought we were going to name her after my mother." He looked puzzled.

"Dora is a nice name, but I named the baby after Leala because she's strong, determined, and a fighter. If you don't mind, I'm tired."

Raj speaks up and says, "You're my wife, and I'm spending the night."

"You can spend the night with the girl you were kissing in the parking lot while I was in labor."

"That's a lie!"

"KJ saw you!" I yelled.

"So you are taking her word over mine?" He asked.

"No, but a picture is worth a thousand words."

I reached over and took KJ's cell phone from the nightstand. Who would have ever thought you could take pictures with your phone? There was Raj in the car with a girl.

"See how your son disrespects me?" I said to his mother.

She was so embarrassed. She said that she was sorry and turned to leave.

"Raj, leave her alone and let's go."

When I got out of the hospital, I went to my mom's house. She cleared out her office and turned it into a nursery for Leala. My room was across the hall. My mother always said that her children would always have a room in her home. When I went into my room, all of my things were still there. It was as if I had never left. Reann came in and told me to stay strong and not to be discouraged because God doesn't make mistakes.

"That beautiful girl will make you want more in life and in love," she said.

Everything was fine for about six months. Leala was healthy, and I was happy to be home. Raj started calling, begging, and crying that he wanted his family back. He said that he didn't have anywhere to go. All I could think about was the fact that Leala needed a father.

When I told my mom, she said, "He cannot live here. Do what you want, but remember that he hasn't been around since Leala was born. He has not changed the first diaper, fed her one bottle, or been to one doctor's appointment. Lurleen he hasn't even called to make sure she or you are still alive. Think about it!"

My brother Freddy and his wife took Leala for the weekend. I needed to get out for a while. I went to the mall, walked around, and window shopped. I went to the bookstore and ordered some coffee. I sat down to read a few magazines. I looked up, and Raj was looking pitiful and holding a bear and some bags from Baby Gap. He came over and sat down at my table.

"Give me another chance. I miss you. Let me take you to dinner tonight. No matter what, you are still my wife."

I glared at him. "I don't want dinner, but I do want a divorce."

"I'm not giving you a divorce. Just forget it!"

"You haven't called in six months. What do you think I'm supposed to do? Stay in marriage with a man that is being intimate with other women? What kind of marriage is that? I'm giving you freedom to do whatever or whomever you want to do. Go away, Raj!"

I felt so empowered when he left. I didn't even feel bad or cry. I finished my coffee and called my mom. I told her what happened and that I needed some time to myself. I was going to a late movie, and I would be home later. She told me to be careful.

After the movie as I walked to my car, I heard someone calling my name. It was Raj. How did he know where I was? I felt uneasy. I was trying to get into my car as quickly as possible, but he grabbed me and put a gun to my stomach.

"Say one word, and Leala won't have a mother or father because I'll kill us both. Get into the car and slide over, I'm driving."

He took me back to his apartment. He had music playing, and I thought to myself, *I hope he doesn't think that I'm going to sleep with him.*

"Raj, I need to call home. Mom is expecting me after the movie."

"You are a grown woman, my woman, and you are staying with me.

My mind and heart were racing.

He turned to me and said, "We're going to make love to make up for the lost time."

"No, Raj! I don't want to. Not like this."

"You will because you are my wife!"

At that point, he slapped me to the ground and ripped my shirt open and started to kiss my chest. I begged him to stop, but he didn't. I reached for the vase and swung at him, hitting him on the shoulder.

"You've done it now!" he yelled.

He hit me again. He tore the zipper of my pants as he fought to pull them off. I kicked him and tried to make my way to the door. At this point, all I had on was my bra and one leg in my pants. He grabbed me by the back of my hair and threw me to the ground. He held me by my throat as he thrust himself inside me over and over again. I kept pleading for him to stop.

He was yelling, "You're still my wife!" He kept going until he reached climax and fell on top of me.

Crying hysterically, I begged him not to hurt me again.

"Shut up!" he yelled as he hit me again.

My lips felt like they blew up right away. I could taste blood inside my mouth. Raj pushed himself inside my torn and aching body.

"Why are you doing this?"

He just kept on and on until my whole body went numb and lifeless. When he was finished, he started to cry and rolled off me.

He whispered, "I love you, Lurleen. I'm so sorry. I don't know what happened to me. Your keys are on the table."

I thought that this was a trick, and he was going to attack me again, but he got up, went into the bedroom and closed the door.

My body was so torn, beat, and hurt that I could barely move. I put my pants on and held my shirt together. As soon as I opened the door, I heard Raj yell, "Just go home. Things got out of hand. If I go to jail, things will only be worse next time." Does he think I can act like nothing happened?

I sped off and went to the first medical facility I saw. I could hardly get out of the car, thankfully, a nurse saw me and grabbed a wheelchair. They asked for my name and number. I got on the table, and the questions began. I told them I was kidnapped and raped by my husband. The doctor did a series of tests and then gave me a strong painkiller. I fell asleep, and when I woke up my mom, sister and brothers were sitting around my bed.

Willie said, "Raj has been arrested."

The doctor came in and told me that most of my tests came back negative, but I had gonorrhea. The other test results wouldn't be in for a few more weeks. He indicated that they wanted to keep me overnight and that I really needed to get some rest.

Mom said, "Hold hands and let's pray."

She prayed for divine will for my life now through the pain of this stepping stone. My family left. I lay in my room clicking the channels. I saw Juanita Bynum talking about trials and tribulations and how they will make you stronger. I must have fallen asleep because I dreamt that I was on stage talking to a large room full of women. I was strong and courageous. When I woke up, I realized that that the Lord had revealed my calling to me.

I called my friend, Lyric. I remembered that she too had been raped at a young age, but her healing had not taken place yet. When I got out of the hospital, I went home to a wonderful family and a beautiful baby girl. Leala is the reason I'm determined to make a difference in someone's life.

My outer healing took two months, but my inner healing was requiring action. The Word of God and my church gave me strength to move forward with my life. Lyric and I formed a group called True Healing of a Woman. We became activists for violence against women. Lyric and I co-wrote a book "The Gift in the Struggle," it empowers women to move past tribulation and trouble to create the life that we all deserve to live.

It's been five years, and Leala is in kindergarten. My friends are successful. Lyric and I have a non-profit organization called 'Silent No More' stationed all over the country. Raj is still promising to beat me down, but I am strong and unafraid of his threats.

You never know which road life will push you down. You just need to have the courage to keep on stepping.

THE BATTLE BETWEEN HOLINESS AND FLESH

Leaders, Your Secret Battles can Affect
the Souls of the Church

Pastor Isom was a great man of God with a beautiful wife. He came in working hard to put the church in a positive light with the community and other churches.

New Testimonial went through a horrible breakdown when our old pastor left for no reason. It broke the hearts of all the members, but I personally understood his frustrations with the church of closed minds. Nevertheless, it was still a miserable feeling to watch such a wonderful man be destroyed by people. I prayed for God to bless us with someone that was down to earth and could understand the people who were just trying so hard to be better.

There is nothing worse than a pastor who thinks he hung the moon and had never fallen short of the glory of God. Anyway, I was thankful that one of the Elders found Pastor Isom. We would have a leader, and all of the little pastors in the church can just have a seat.

Pastor Isom came in the spring of 2009, and our church has grown and developed into the young adult church of the city. He had a way about himself that just drew the young and the young at heart. One Sunday after church, I heard Pastor calling me from his office.

"Evangelist Celeste, can you come in here for a moment?"

"Yes, Sir Pastor!"

I got in the office, and he had such a distraught look on his face.

He said, "I have been presented with a challenge. I need to put together a group of at least five preachers to speak on the Miracles of the Supernatural Healing Power of God."

"What do you need me to do to help you?" I asked.

"Can you please get the Evangelist and Ministers together and offer them the opportunity but if no one volunteers, you pick five?"

Whoa, Pastor! You know these folks. If I do not choose the right one, my head is on the chopping block.

"Evangelist, it is not like you aren't offering them an opportunity to volunteer. Everyone wants to preach on Sunday morning, but no one wants to help any other time."

I could hear and see the frustration of the pastor for the first time since he has been here.

"Don't worry about it, Pastor. Just send me the time and date, and I will have five people in place. Will you be there?

No, I have a prior engagement on the same day.

No problem, I got it!" I said assuredly.

After Bible study the following Wednesday, I got everyone together and presented the opportunity for them to help the pastor with this program at our sister church. I thought that it would be an easy flow of conversation and agreement, but no everyone wanted to preach in front of the Apostle of the movement. I remembered the look on Pastor Isom's face during our meeting and decided to just get aggressive with these people of God.

Out of nowhere, I heard myself say, "Okay, since we cannot come to a decision when I call your name stand up and wait for instructions. Minister Taylor."

He stood up, and I said, "Give me a two-minute message on the topic." He fumbled profusely but made a great effort.

"Evangelist Moore?" She stood up and gave the most eloquent two minutes of a divine and prophetic word.

You know after one person does their thing everyone tried to show out then but what they failed to realize was that I was looking for content not screaming and yelling hype. Out of ten messages, I chose the five I thought were the most compelling and heartfelt. Boy, oh boy, was my name mud after that meeting. I did not care. I wanted to make sure that the best representatives of God were presented to our Apostle. People will whoop and holler over anything, but my goal was to make sure that a word of change, deliverance and the Holy Spirit was represented. I did the best I could to make sure that everyone understood and left the meeting with a peaceful frame of mind.

I called the pastor on Thursday morning and let him know the names of the chosen five.

"Thank you so much, Evangelist Celeste. You have no idea how thankful I am that you made this happen."

"Pastor, are you all right? You sound kind of strained."

He immediately said, "No, I am fine Celeste."

"Okay, will you be at choir practice tonight?"

"No, Evangelist. I will not."

"Hey, what is going on Pastor? You have a solo on Sunday."

"I know; I will have it in perfect harmony."

Hmmm. My thoughts were all over the place once we hung up the phone. Is he sick?

I went on about my business, and I noticed that the following Sunday the message was so meaningful and thought provoking. It was about being obedient to the voice of God. Beautiful! Pastor Isom seemed to be back to normal. He was outside with the youth kicking the soccer ball in the field after church.

Our church was beautifully located on about five acres of land. Since Pastor Isom had been there, we decided to extend the church to add more bathrooms, a second kitchen, and room for arts and crafts. The big project was to allow space for the young men to learn carpentry and build furniture. The pastor had so many ideas and plans for our youth. Truly letting the old men teach the young men about life. Working on furniture allowed them to be creative and put their heart into their furniture. This was an exciting time for New Testimonial Church.

The pastor's wife was a unique lady. She could preach, sing, cook and teach but sometimes she seemed a little off for her position. It was weird to me. I asked First Lady Isom if she wanted to help the women's group with the mission drive. We had an opportunity to send clothes and toiletries to Honduras on behalf of our sister church's mission trip to help with the kids over there. We were a month out, and it was really time to get on the ball of asking the members to bring in items.

I called First Lady to ask her thoughts about the drive, and she said, "Evangelist Celeste, can you get with the Mothers and some of the other ladies to get the list of needs together? Then we will announce it next week at Bible Study."

"Yes, Ma'am, I can do that and give it to Sister Ida for the bulletin.

"Thank you so much!"

Last night Pastor Isom sent a text to remind me to call the five speakers to make sure that they were ready for their ten-minute talk.

"Pastor, you did not tell me a time limit for them so let me make sure no one prepared a full sermon."

"Evangelist that should have been common sense to them. They should know they would only have a small amount of time. There are five speakers per church, and three churches are being represented."

I was dead silent because I did not fully understand why he was texting as if I knew there was a time limit. My first thoughts were what in the world was going on with the pastor and First Lady Isom.

I made the individual calls and let the speakers know of the time limit and reminded them of the time of the service. The service was on a Thursday night at 6pm, so we had to cancel choir practice and load up the church van by 5pm because the Church of New Beginnings was about forty-five minutes away.

When we got to the church, the Mothers had fixed a phenomenal meal for us. It was so delicious. I was appointed the mistress of the ceremony, so I had to hurry up and look at the roster and the titles of each message. It was funny to me that our church was the only one that actually produced the five speakers. It was an awesome night; I had a good report to take back to the pastor and First Lady. It felt funny that neither of them was there to support the speakers. When asked where they were, all I could say is that they had a prior engagement.

We were a full year in with our pastor, and it seemed as though everything was going great. However, my spirit was telling me that something was definitely not right with the marriage of our leaders. It is a blessing and a curse that God has given me the gift of prophecy. I have watched them and ignored certain signs of unhappiness between them. They both depend on me a lot to take care of things and make sure that the church is held to the standards of the church doctrine.

I love God, and I have been in the church for a long time. I got saved when I was sixteen, and God blessed me with the gift of sight and prophecy at the age of eighteen. My life has not been an easy one, especially in the love department. I do not have children due to my inability to meet a man that could understand my need to be a blessing to God's people even if it meant being with someone all night during the demons of suicide, loneliness or brokenness. When I was in my twenties, I left the church to see what was out there in the world. What did it mean to spend the night with a man and keep on trucking afterward, like some of the stories I heard my friends talk about at that age? Well, about three years of that mess along with drinking, clubbing, a few drugs, and cursing I was ready to call it quits.

One thing about God is that He gives you free will, but when you have a calling on your life, and He gets tired of your mess, he will provide an eye opening experience to get you back on track if you receive it. My experience was I ended up in the emergency room with alcohol poising and some kind of date rape drug, but God had mercy on me that I was not violated. One of the men recognized me from my youth and I had prayed with him once about his relationship with his family. That was enough for me, so I took my little disobedient self-right back to church, dropped to my knees and asked for forgiveness. I have been with the Lord faithfully ever since. I am about to have my fiftieth birthday in three weeks, and I am eternally thankful that I am still here to see it. Amen!

The church is doing so well, and it is filled with young people more and more every Sunday and at Wednesday night Bible study. It is amazing because we couldn't get a young person to stay faithful in this church until Pastor Isom came, so we are rejoicing. The Deacons and Elders have new sparks in their eyes and are at every service. They are taking time out with the youth. Some of them are going to their games and attending their musical events. The First Lady seems to be more into the groups to help the girls learn how to be true ladies. She is teaching our older girls how to dress in the corporate world. She's also teaching the little ones how to sew and crochet, of all things. It's working because the girls are so excited!

The crochet class is a hit, and now the mothers and daughters are making blankets together for the new babies that come into the church. Beautiful!

The men of the church started to ask the pastor if it was time to start thinking about expanding the church as they had hoped in the beginning.

"Now is not the time," he said.

"Pastor, why?" they asked.

"Don't question me," is the only answer that he gave to them.

One of the Elders came to me on that same Sunday after church and asked me if I had plans for dinner since we did not have a night service that evening. I told him that I did not, so we went to some place called Milestones. It had beautiful décor, and the food was great. We sat there talking about our youth and the things that we needed to get in place for the summer programs.

Elder Jenkins told me about the meeting with the pastor. I usually do not discuss any of my visions with people unless God allows it. I told Elder Jenkins that we must obey the man of God and trust his plan.

Elder said, "Celeste, I honestly do not think that he has a plan anymore. He is distant in all of the Ministers' meetings and anything that has to do with the kids lately he does not seem to have time."

"I did not know this Elder. Let's just pray for a revelation from the Lord and see what happens. If it is something big, I promise you it can't stay hidden for long. Our church is sanctified and blessed. There are enough prayer warriors in the church to turn the entire city around. Look at what is going on with our youth and you men!"

We got through the summer programs, and it was unbelievable. The church even made a profit because kids from neighborhoods near and far came to participate. It got to the point that we had to stop taking applications because of the space that we would need to take care of all of the kids and keep them occupied and fed. Awesome! At the end of the program, we had a huge dinner and celebrated with each child and their families.

The next Sunday morning, there was not an empty seat in the church. Those kids and their parents came back to enjoy our service. The pastor seemed very excited and suggested to me that we find a nice restaurant to have a banquet in for all of the people who participated in teaching the kids during the program. I asked him if he would like First Lady to head this up, and he immediately said, "No! "

"No problem. I got it covered."

After that conversation, I asked the pastor if he would mind if some of us had a prayer lock-in on Friday and he agreed that it was all right. So I got the Mothers, Elders, and Ministers to come and we prayed all night long for God's divine peace to cover our church. I prayed for Gods divine revelation to present itself to me if it was His will. That Sunday, when the folks came in the church, the atmosphere felt renewed and revived. Everything was well.

One of our new young men came up to me during church, hugged me and whispered in my ear, "Can I talk to you now?"

It was during the devotion period, so we went outside, and he had tears in his eyes. I said, "Trent, what's wrong?"

He just reached over and began to weep profusely; I just held him until he could catch his breath, and finally he released our embrace and said, "I need to tell you something."

Honey, you can tell Momma Celeste anything, I won't judge you, but I will help you. You know I am here for you."

He said, "I know you love the pastor and you will do anything to help all of us in this church but.... Pastor Isom and his wife are dirty people."

"What do you mean, love? It is okay, tell me."

Trent wiped his face and looked me straight in the eye and said, "They are swingers and sexual predators of teens."

"Trent, when you say swingers, what do you mean exactly?"

"Momma, they get other adults involved in orgies and swapping partners for the night. If they really like each other, they take trips out of town with that person. If they are in a city where some of the teens that they use live, they will have them join them and pay them off with money, shoes, or clothes."

"Trent, I need you, to be honest with me, look at me, son. Have they done anything to you?"

The look on his face told me that something had happened. As we sat there in silence, he finally said, "Yes."

We sat in silence for a minute. He didn't want to talk any more about it at the moment.

"Ok, do you want to go back into the church or would you like me to take you home?"

He said, "Elder Jenkins is preaching today, and I want to hear him."

Then out of the clear blue sky, he said, "Momma, you know he likes you."

"I like him too. Trent, he is a great man of God and has been faithful to the church."

"Momma come down for a minute. He likes you and wants to like a date with you or marry you."

"Boy, why would you say that?"

"A man knows another man and I'm telling you; he is into you." We both laughed.

I was so proud of Trent for being able to tell me something so devastating and then to say something that made me smile. No one ever really does that for me. They dump on me and leave, but this baby did a

Momma Celeste, I will always love him for that moment.

Now, what do I do with this information? I had suspected something was wrong with this couple, but I was so wrapped up in helping the church, and it's growth. My focus was on making sure that all of the needs were met, and everything met all of the standards of the doctrine and the state since we had a day care and summer program in the works. Why did the Lord not let me have a vision about the leaders? I had negative feelings, but I thought it was because they were so young and needed to become used to the success of the ministry.

I honestly believed that my calling was to take care of the people that came through the door of the church. Make sure that if they needed clarification of the word or just someone to talk to, I could help the pastor. One Saturday, I asked the First Lady if she would like to have breakfast with me since we had not had any time together in months. I really just wanted to see if she needed anything.

She said, "Evangelist Celeste, I appreciate all that you do here but you are just a helper to the ministry, and it appears to me that the church considers you to be the end all be all of the church."

I was thrown for a loop. "I do apologize for this perception, but I promise you my intentions and my heart is only to serve the people of God. I am here for everyone. Since I do not have a family, the church is my family. What would you like me to do First Lady to help ease this tension that seems to be between us right now?"

This woman said to me, "Leave the church and let me take my position here."

"Hmmm, that is pretty harsh, First Lady. I have been at this church since my twenties and have seen ten pastors come through here. The Lord told me to be a blessing to the leaders of this church, and He would let me know when my season is over. So unless you bring me before the pastor and the Apostles of this movement to have me removed from this church, we need to figure out how to work together for the good of the people of God."

I was so taken aback from this conversation that I really needed to share this with someone I trusted. I thought about what my sweet Trent told me about Elder Jenkins, we have always been able to talk about the church but today I really just wanted to hang out with someone. I called him, and he didn't answer. Immediately I thought, oh well it wasn't meant for me to do that, so I will take myself out for dinner and a movie. It wasn't ten minutes after I made that decision the phone rang, and it was Elder Jenkins.

"Sorry Celeste, I was in the store trying to figure out something for dinner. It is so beautiful outside today. I wanted to put a steak on the grill, but it's not always fun to grill only for myself."

I thought to myself, *Okay, I think that was an opening.*

"Elder I was calling to see if you would like to have dinner with me today."

The phone went dead silent, "Hello?"

His voice chimed in," Celeste where would you like to go or would you like to come here? I can grill, and we can watch a movie if you like. Which would you like to do Celeste?"

"Ok. I will come there, would you like for me to bring anything or rent a movie?"

"Just bring yourself, I got it all covered. You don't like tomatoes, do you?"

I giggled, "How do you know that?"

"I have been at hundreds of dinners with you, and I have never seen you eating tomatoes. I just wanted to make sure that I did not put any in the salad." I smiled. That was so cute to me.

I put on a pretty sundress and cute, comfy shoes. I was looking forward to an evening of conversation with someone that really did not expect or need anything from me. I did not realize how much I put myself on the back burner for the peace and happiness of others. I have never been past the front door of the Elder's house, so I was a little nervous.

This man has been my friend for many years, so I don't really know why I was jittery.

When I pulled into the driveway, I could see the smoke coming up from behind a wooden fence. He came out to meet me with a glass of sweet tea in his hand. He opened the gate, and I was amazed at how beautiful everything was in the yard. Elder had a beautiful area with the grill, nice tables, chairs and a pool. There was a smooth jazz piece playing in the background.

"Celeste, I am so happy that you are here. The steaks have a little while to cook, would you like a tour of the house?

"Sure," I replied.

We went up on the deck that was screened in; the table was set up for two with flowers and place settings. There were lanterns strung up in the ceiling of the deck. We went into the kitchen, and it was like stepping into "Better Homes and Gardens." Everything was black and stainless steel. The faucets were beautiful, and all of the sunlight made the kitchen a dream kitchen in my book. We went into the living room, and it was modern and comfortable with cream colored furniture and a lot of lamps, vases, and photos.

"This is my guest suite."

"Wow! It is beautiful." I said admiringly.

And then he opened the door to his bedroom and said, "Take a look."

"Oh, my!"

He has the two-sided fireplace that goes into the bedroom, and the other side is in the bathroom. Then on top of everything he has a beautiful covered patio with a fireplace and sixty inch TV off from the master. I was astonished because he is so humble and he never bragged or boasted. The front of the house does not look as if it was this big or immaculate.

After the tour, he said, "So what do you think?"

"It is amazing and beautiful."

"It would be better if I had someone to share it with but for now it is just me."

We went back to the screened porch.

"Have a seat Ms. C and let me check on the steaks and vegetables."

When he came back, he said, "We are almost done let me bring out the rest of the food."

"Do you want me to help?"

"No lady, let someone take care of you for a change."

I sat back in my seat and enjoyed the cool breeze, the perfectly made tea and the smell of a delicious meal that I did not have to prepare.

The Elder came back with chilled shrimp cocktail for an appetizer, and then he brought out the salads. He strolled to the grill and plated up our steaks, asparagus, zucchini, and squash. He even had some brown sugar pineapples on the grill that he laid on top of my steak as a garnishment. Pineapples are my favorite fruit. That was so sweet. We sat outside and talked and ate for at least three hours.

"Elder I need to ask you something and then tell you something."

"Celeste, I need you to call me by my first name when we are together. My name is Seth. Please call me that from this point on okay."

"I didn't want to be disrespectful and not call you Elder."

"Girl that is a title and is not my birth name. We will not get tied up in titles. We will work within them, but we are still individuals, call me Seth. Now that we are clear on that, would you like to go inside for this conversation?" I bought some gelato and lemon cake."

"Sure," I said.

We went into the den, and it had the same music playing in there as outside. This man is totally cool with me. I checked the time, and it was barely 6pm, so I felt comfortable staying for a little while longer. I took my shoes off and sat cross-legged on this huge comfy chair with a blanket over my legs. It felt like I was at home.

"Anyway, do you think that I try to take over the church from the new leaders?"

"What kind of question is that lady? You do all you can to assist them in maintaining the church and the members. You are there all the time so the people know they can depend on you. It's not your fault that they are not there as much as they once were when they started."

It was funny to me that Seth did not ask me who said that to me, he just started speaking to me as if he already knew.

"Do you think that I have a takeover spirit?"

"No, Celeste, you have the spirit of a servant leader. Non-judgmental and loving to those in need and a comfort to those that needs encouragement. If someone doesn't like it, let them leave."

Wow! He was ticked, so I knew something had been said in his presence. I looked at him and really wanted to hug him, but I refrained. At that time, I felt the need to tell him that the First Lady asked me to leave the church. When that sentence came out of my mouth, he just got up and came over and sat with me in the big chair and put his arm around me. I leaned on his shoulder and cried. I loved God, and I knew that I have never had any ill intentions in my heart to make any leader feel as though I was trying to take over. While I was there in such a safe space, I told Seth about the information I received from Trent.

He jumped up and said, "Celeste that explains it, and he just paced the floor."

He grabbed my hand and said, "Let's pray for them right now."

He prayed a while, and I prayed awhile. We prayed for God to reveal their wicked ways in a way that it would not destroy the people of God but help them to understand the battles of living holy and having unresolved addictions. They will not leave the church but will be relieved that God has exposed the enemy for our betterment and growth. We carried and prayed for wisdom for our next step in the ministry. I left about 8pm. It was the summer, so it was still light outside. I got home and thought about the evening, and my heart was happy, safe and grateful.

Sunday morning Pastor Isom and his wife were in the pulpit, and they had the strangest look on their faces. The church was not at peace, and you could feel it.

Trent came over to me and said, "Momma, I am going to talk to you later. I will not listen to them speak about anything. I will be by to cut your grass on Monday after I get off work."

I couldn't convince him to stay, but I totally understood. The choir was off today, and there was no spirit in the sanctuary. I looked at Elder Jenkins, and he held his finger up to his mouth as if to tell me to wait or to be quiet, so I just sat there and tried to get into the service. The next thing I knew the Apostles from the movement walked through the door along with the police. I was stunned. What is going on? All of the Apostles sat down on the first pew and just looked at the pulpit.

Pastor Isom jumped up and said, "Saints of God. I need to share something with you that I am utterly ashamed to have taken part in and for the rest of my life I will be sorry."

He looked at our youth and said, "You can make mistakes in life; that is how you learn, but when you are a man and woman of God in leadership, you should know how to live and be an example for your youth and your church as a whole."

He looked over at his wife and said, "Young men never let the wiles of a woman be your demise."

One of the Apostles stood up and told Pastor Isom to get on with the explanations of sin.

The pastor took a deep breath and said, "People of God, there is a secret battle between holiness and the flesh that I have been faced with for years, and this is the first time that I will confess my sins before those that I have and will hurt. I will not be confessing anything for the woman that I am married to as we must be responsible for our own soul salvation. I have a sickness in my flesh that I can't control. I am weak when it comes to sex, and I really don't know how to control it, and now I have disappointed the people of God and myself."

Pastor Isom looked so defeated and sorry for his actions. He looked at his wife and offered her the podium.

This lady looked at him and said, "I have not done anything wrong, and I will not be confessing anything today."

Before the Apostle could stand up to say anything, I heard a voice behind me screaming, "What about what you made me do?"

I turned to see Trent standing in the church doorway. I thought he was gone, but there he was with Elder Jenkins at his side. The Apostle stood up and asked him to come to the front of the church.

"Young man tell us what you know."

"You had better keep that mouth closed Trent!" the First Lady yelled with fire in her eyes.

Even Pastor Isom looked confused.

Trent began to weep as he screamed, "Who is in control now?"

He looked at the church and began to tell us how the "Woman of God" had been paying him, bribing him, to have sex with her. She, in turn, would tell the college recruiter that was a friend of hers to look at him for the promised basketball scholarship.

"I will be the first person in my home to go to college, and I did not want to disappoint my family, so I endured this sin that I knew was wrong for the sake of an opportunity that I felt at the time another person had control over. When I told Elder Jenkins about this mess, he said that God is in control and asked me did I want this woman to have new opportunities to violate my brothers in the church? That is why I came forward."

Pastor Isom jumped back up and said, "See young men, I laid down my life for the wiles of a woman, and it was still not enough."

He began to tell the church the entire truth. "We set up a ring of married sexual swingers and teenagers that would participate throughout the movement, but they were never to use the teens or people from this church."

He fell to the floor in such agony and grief that my soul cried out for the man. I looked at the woman as she stood there with no remorse and called him weak and childlike. This is the battle between holiness and addiction within a marriage.

My Lord, was my heart grieving as I looked at the faces of the youth and the people of God. Then the Lord began to show me those that had been violated. I did not say a word but began to pray that their spirits would be able to be free today. The Apostles stood up and turned to the congregation and asked if anyone else had been involved with the woman. The very ones that I saw stood up. Ten young men sixteen to eighteen years old wept in embarrassment, and I just wanted to go and hold all of them as the tears rolled down their faces.

I looked at Elder Jenkins hoping that he could hear my heart call to him. I thought I was going to start screaming at the possibility of all of the faith, trust and dreams of being good men and leaders in the church stood on the threshold of being flushed into a sea of forgetfulness by these ten young leaders. I put my head down and silently cried never dropping one tear, but there was a sea of tears raging in my soul. When I held my head up Elder Jenkins was standing right beside me. All I could do was look at him and silently thank him for being so dear and caring in the midst of this mess.

The Apostle told the pastor and his wife to come out of the pulpit and come to the front of the church. The four of them went to the platform, and our founder of the movement began to speak.

He said, "Your behavior is disappointing. In all my years in church, I have never experienced this type of situation. God is faithful to restore you if you want your soul to be restored to the order of God. He can do it, and He can keep you if you want to be kept. Pastor Isom, once I was informed of this, we hired a private investigator to begin a case; because of the growth of your church and the other churches in the movement, I did not want to ruin the souls of the people. We did not want the children to be hurt from the addictions of yourself and your wife so every time over the past month that a meeting was set up with a teen in any city, they could not make it. The adults, they had a choice and knew the word of God, but we protected the teens first. There were no bribes being given to the adults. Therefore, their addictions were their choices. As of this day, at each church, the forty people that are involved in this situation are all being escorted from the church."

He continued, "All of the church money was accounted for at every church. We can't charge you with anything because of the serpent-like wisdom of seeking teens that were considered legal in the sight of the law. We are speaking to each one to make sure their experience with you all did not happen earlier than the age of sixteen. At this time you are released from this church, the movement, and your positions. The paperwork has been drawn up for your signatures. You were not charged by the law, but the battle of addiction is a silent killer, so we pray that you all get help and find peace for your soul."

As of this day, Elder Jenkins will become the pastor of this church. He has labored in faith, love, and consistency since he walked through these doors twenty plus years ago. The church went from a gulf of tears of pain, and betrayal to a roar of joy! Trent came and stood beside me as the Elder was escorted to the pulpit and how proud I was that the church did not have an opportunity to fall apart and dismantle because of the behavior of the pastor and his wife.

After church, I sat in the sanctuary and loved on those that felt betrayed, but I was also happy all in the same breath. When the church was completely empty, Trent and I were cleaning up and listening to music.

"Momma Celeste, sit down with me for a minute. Thank you, for being here with me throughout this situation."

"Trent, I did not know what was happening to you."

"I am glad you did not, or I would have never been able to see the grace of God on people that hurt others. God loves us through all of our mess, but He will allow it to be uncovered if you don't stop. So I am glad you didn't use that radar vision that God gave you on this."

"But Trent, I feel like I sinned because I did not feed into the feelings that I was having. I focused on the souls that were coming in, but I knew deep down something was wrong."

"I know you are not blaming yourself! Good grief momma, give yourself a break sometimes! Anyway, this is what I really wanted to say..."

"Wait! Did you just yell at me, boy?"

"Ummm, I think I did, but it was in love." We laughed.

Trent looked me in my eyes and said, "I need you to allow someone to replenish the love that you so freely give to others."

"God does that for me daily," I replied.

"Ugh! Momma, come out of the spirit for a second and go with me. Everyone needs someone to love and be one with. It is your time to let your guard down to love and have someone to do things for you and with you. You need someone to cry with, laugh with, cook for, cook for you. Do you feel where I am going with this?"

"I do son."

"Right momma, you do. Now Elder Jenkins is in the banquet hall, and he would like to see you for a minute."

I got there, and he had a bouquet of roses.

"Hey, Seth."

"Hey Celeste, come over and sit with me."

He said, "I know this is not crazy romantic but I am about to burst, and I need to do this now. We have been friends for twenty-five or so years, and I have loved you with my entire heart for the last six. This is the seventh year, and seven is a perfect number of completion. My life is wonderful, but it would be complete if I could have you in it every day, every month, every year, in every way and call you Mrs. Seth Jenkins. You know Elder Jenkin's ole lady." We both burst out laughing, but I was really crying and laughing.

He dropped down on one knee, and at that moment a beautiful jazz piece came over the speaker, and it was so sweet and soft.

He asked, "Will you marry me?"

I didn't have to pray about it, think about it, and meditate on it.

I said, "Yes!"

He put the most beautiful ring on my finger and if the truth be told it was the very ring that I always wanted. It was a monster ring too, five karats. Yikes! He loves me, and I love him. We are in one accord, and God is first.

God will be faithful to you if you are faithful to him.

Dying in Silence

The Double Life of Love

Life is so ridiculous sometimes, but we have to believe that everything is divinely purposed. If it is divinely purposed, then why has my heart been destroyed more times than I can count? After a separation in my spirit and four kids to raise pretty much on my own, faith in what love was supposed to be was pretty much non-existent in my heart and soul. When it came to someone genuinely loving me for me, my entire life, from childhood to this day has been one disappointment after another.

By the time I met my husband, Jacob, I was so tired of life's disappointments. When he asked me to marry him, I was like, okay dude, that's cool. Did I love him? Yes. Was I in love with him? Not so much. Jacob was a man of fun and laughter, but when life goes serious, this man disappeared not just physically but mentally. He acted like everything was okay and would leave the hard work up to me. Is that the way this was supposed to work? I was pretty confident that it was not. Jacob wanted to go to the club, shoot pool, gamble and come home whenever he got good and ready. What the hell was I thinking? I married this man out of a selfish need to be loved and the need to let someone else take care of me for a change. Boy, did I have the wrong vision?

By the way, my name is Sincere Star Ryan. I love my name, but I promise you that I have never felt like a star because of my harsh background, present troubles, and things are not looking too promising for the future. Being that my parents do not believe in divorce, it looks like I am going to be trapped in this eternal hell until I die. On the flip side, my kids are amazing, and I love them very much. Cody is the oldest; he is seventeen and an old soul. He can pick up when my emotions were all over the place and when I am about to snap.

On those special days, I could hear him saying, "Okay guys, it's Big Brother Day. Let's pack up the car for an outing."

I loved him so much for that wisdom. His twin brother Collin, on the other hand, was more of a technical person who would rather be left alone with his thoughts and electronics. Those last two, Summer and Stormy, oh my goodness! They are partners in crime. These girls acted so much alike that sometimes I could not even tell them apart. They were fifteen going on twenty-five and trying to keep them contained within the rules of the house was a feat for all of us to take on. Overall our home was filled with a wonderfully eclectic range of personalities, hopes, and dreams. When Jacob was home, the dynamics of the house was off for me, but he did treat the kids with love. It was just me that he seemed determined to make feel alone and unloved.

Love is something that I have longed for my entire life. When I was younger, I had a great boyfriend whom I thought loved me but as soon as he went to college, not a word from him again, nothing. I lost my virginity to him and everything. I thought that my heart would never heal from that loss.

I went on to college and met Harlan Armstrong; he was handsome, smart, and very attentive to me. He was so romantic and found time for me every day even though he was on the debate team and student government organization. He spoke several different languages, and those classes kept him pretty busy. He was a Criminal Justice major and minor in Business because he wanted to own his own practice after working with a firm for a few years. I just knew that we were a perfect match as I was a Criminal Law major also. We were so busy but never too busy for each other. We understood each other and the schedules. He totally gets me, I thought. We stayed together throughout our junior and senior years of college and graduated together. No one could have told me that we were not going to be married and be the power couple of the century. We had the most enchanted graduation evening. He rented a yacht, and we enjoyed the beautiful weather and a scrumptious meal.

I thought, *Oh my goodness, this is it, he is going to ask me to marry him.* My soul craved to belong to a committed relationship and to know that we would be there for each other no matter what. After a beautiful night of love and promises, when I woke up the yacht was docked, and he was gone. I thought he went to pick up something, maybe a gift, because the note on the pillow said *enjoy your breakfast, love you.* So I dressed, went to the deck, and a beautiful breakfast was prepared. The attendant was there to make sure all was well with me. After I had finished eating, enjoying the weather and the music playing, I was so relaxed but still in a bit of anticipation on him returning. Finally, Captain Shawn came up and asked if he could have a seat.

"Sure, I would love the company, especially since I have no idea where Harlan went so early this morning."

Captain Shawn had this look on his face like he had something to say. I asked him if he was all right and he proceeded to tell me that Harlan would not be coming back to the yacht.

"May I ask why?"

"He left you this note."

"A note!"

I opened the note to only read that he had been dating Marissa the Delta for the last year of our relationship and he was going to marry her in three weeks. I thought my heart would stop beating. Why in the world would he go through this wonderful night of love and memories to leave me with a memory of abandonment and betrayal? Why would he do this to me? He said that he loved me.

I tried to call him, but the number was disconnected. Captain Shawn looked as though this pain happened to him and offered a hug. I did not want it because I did not know him, but pain recognizes pain, so I fell into his arms and sobbed like a baby. When I finally released him and looked at him to thank him he was also sobbing.

I said, "I did not know that we were staying on this yacht after graduation, so I don't have anything clean to put on."

"You have a hang-up bag in the bathroom with clothes and shoes. On the bed are your unmentionables laid out for you," he replied.

"There is a driver here, to take you home or wherever you need to go. He has been paid to take you around all day if you need him to."

"Thank you for your kindness and allowing me to fall apart on your nice white shirt."

He laughed and asked if I ever needed to talk I could feel free to contact him at any time and gave me his card. My first thought was to toss it in the river, but I just smiled, went to shower and dressed.

Harlan did not pack clothes from my apartment; he bought me new everything down to my shoes and perfume. There was a credit card in the bag with a card that *said I am so sorry Sincere; I have enclosed a credit card with five thousand dollars on it to help with any expenses you may have during the transition period from school to job. It's not much, but I felt I needed to do something for you.* I failed to mention that Harland Armstrong came from a family of money.

The driver must have known of my great pain also because his eyes grieved with my heart. How horrible to have this experience and to be left here alone with two men that I did not even know to help me through the first five hours of it. I asked the driver to take me to Harlan's apartment. I got my keys out and opened the door. Everything was gone; nothing was left except the echo from the squeal of pain from the pit of my stomach. I whaled so loudly that the driver came in and sat on the floor with me and just watched me wrench in an uncontrollable cry, I could not understand why this was happening to me. I thought I was enough for any man, but I wasn't enough for him.

I guess the driver could not take it another minute.

"Can I hold you, Ms. Star?"

Without hesitation, I said, "Yes."

I scooted over to him, and we just sat there in silence except for the occasional spontaneous combustion of tears. This man has just held me through darn near vomiting on him, so I asked his name.

He answered, "Jacob Ryan."

All of the sudden, my stomach started to growl so loud. It was embarrassing!

"Would you like to go and get something to eat? My treat".

I responded, "No, it will be Harlan's treat. How about that? What's your favorite food, Jacob?"

"Seafood."

"Mines too. Let's go!"

I locked the door back. Jacob put me in the car and off we went. We stopped at some seafood place right off the ocean that I had never been to before. They caught my lobster and cooked it at that moment. It was incredible. Jacob got the crab legs. They were the biggest crab legs I had ever seen in my life! We had some drinks and listened to the live reggae band that was playing. It was a lovely evening.

Jacob took me home about 7:30. I almost asked him to come up, but I did not want to act like a hooker. I was feeling really nice after a few drinks, and he was such great company.

"Sincere, may I kiss you?" He asked.

"I don't think that would be a good idea at this moment but here is my number, you can check on me every now and then if you'd like." He walked me to the door and gave me a hug and left.

When I opened the door to my apartment, there was a box in the middle of the floor. I just looked at it and began to strip down to my undies. I seem to think better that way when I am upset. I grabbed a robe and went to my balcony and sat down to view the beautiful river and listen to all of the laughter of my neighbors who were having a little gathering up under me.

As I sat there and looked at the river and the ripples from the boats, I wondered if I would ever be able to have the same love for the beauty and peacefulness of the water again. I began to weep profusely. My neighbors started telling everyone to be quiet and started calling my name, so I went inside.

I slipped inside and put on some saxophone jazz and ran me a lavender bath. Should I open this box now or wait until I am relaxed? I know it was my things from Harland's apartment. I may as well get it over with, so I picked up the box and went to the couch. As soon as I opened it, a card was on top. I opened it up, and it was from Harland's mother and father; talk about ultimate betrayal! These two darn near put me in their will, but now they are going to celebrate their son's wedding with a woman that is the total opposite of me. How the hell does that work, was all I could say to myself. Inside the card was a photo of me with his family. Huh? Why would they send me this?

I threw it down, and something fell out of the card. It was a fat stack of cash and a card full of I am sorry that we hurt you notes. Then on the bottom were all of my things from his apartment. Taped to the bottom of the box was a box with a locket inside with both of our graduation photos in it. It was inscribed, *this love will never die*. Why in the world would the do this to me? Harlan wasn't man enough to tell me to my face that he was in love with another woman and that I was not good enough for him.

See in my mind that is all that I hear after all of the things that I have been through within the last 48 hours. I was abandoned again by someone that I thought loved me with his whole heart and soul but in reality, he did not. All I see is men leaving me for no reason that I could understand. Betrayal from people that I thought loved me. Again, the very thing that I want more than anything has escaped my grasp again.

Crap! My bath is running; I made it just in time. I let a little water out and grabbed me the biggest glass of wine I could pour and sank my body into the tub. I drank and cried. I brought the bottle in the bathroom, so I guzzled and sobbed until the water was cold. My cell phone had rung about eight times. I grabbed my towel, dried off a little and went to find that stupid phone. D

Dang, it was my mom. I forgot that I had not spoken to her since the graduation. She is totally screaming at me because she did not know where I was for thirty-six hours. I let her do her thing before saying, "So how are you mom besides being ticked off at me?"

"Harland's parents have been calling me trying to see if you were okay. What happened Sincere?"

"You mean they did not tell you? That is surprising. Momma, how about I come and pick you up and take you to dinner or something? Whatever you want to do let's just have a date."

"Sincere, do you realize that we did not celebrate your graduation."

"Well, we will do it in about an hour or so how about that?"

"What about your Father?"

"What about him? I am taking you out; you deal with that mess."

My father left me when I was a child and just came back home my sophomore year of college. I got nothing for the man.

"He is not there now anyway. Right?"

Momma whispered, "No, he is not here."

"Put your clothes on momma; I will be there in an hour."

That was cool; I needed to get out of this house anyway. I can't let momma see my pain because she will try to fix it and I am not in the mood to be fixed today. I want to suffer in silence and then try to pull myself together. That is how I roll!

I picked momma up, and we did everything from massage, manicures, pedicures, and dinner. I, of course, did not drink a thing because of my wine drinking competition in the bathtub earlier. As soon as I dropped her off the King of abandonment, my dad shows up trying to talk to me. Since I did come from his sperm, I tried to be cordial. I hugged them both and got the heck out of there.

Good grief I have had enough of this freaking day. I am going to bed. I turned on my favorite show "Scandal" and watched it until I fell asleep. The next morning, I heard my doorbell ringing. It was a florist. There was a huge bouquet of flowers that covered the delivery person's face.

He said, "Sincere Star, please."

"That would be me."

"This monstrosity of flowers is for you. They are so heavy. Do you want me to bring them in and sit them down somewhere?"

"If you don't mind that would be great." I signed the form and looked at the card. It was from Jacob Ryan.

Wow! This guy is working on me while he thinks I am venerable. What he doesn't know about me is that I have been hurt, disappointed and abandoned so much in my life that I, unfortunately, look for something to go wrong even when everything feels so good and right. I called him and asked him if he would like to meet for breakfast.

He asked, "At your place or out."

"Out! Buddy," I laughed.

"I know that girl I am just trying to make you laugh. So where would you like to meet? How about Cracker Barrel on Mayflower and are you dressed or will it be another hour?"

"Dude, I am the fastest dresser in the west. See you in twenty."

"My kind of woman. See you in a minute."

I still beat him to the restaurant, slow poke. I had an obsessive relationship with Cracker Barrel pancakes, so I ordered a big stack with turkey sausage and two eggs.

"You are surely not going to eat all of that."

"I surely am and don't judge me." I laughed. "I only come here once a month for this good old fattening stuff, and I am going to get some root beer barrels when we leave."

We had the best time at breakfast. From that point on we were inseparable for about a year. One Thursday morning Jacob and I were both off work. Yes, in the midst of all of the crap I followed my dreams and started working for Phipps and Styles Law Firm. I was working my way up the ranks pretty good and was ahead of my five-year plan. Jacob knew how much I adored waterfalls, so we did a five-mile round-trip hike. In the middle of the walk was an incredible waterfall that was on full blast.

He pointed, "Let's sit on the rock over by the fall."

He put down our backpacks and pulled out some waters and some protein bars. He took some pictures of me near the falls and then we took some selfies. He is so funny.

"What a perfect day today! I have enjoyed this so much, honey." I said with a big smile on my face.

I was trying to find a piece of gum in my backpack because to kiss with protein on your breath is terrible. When I turned around, he was on one knee.

"You okay, babe?" I asked.

"Sincere do you love me?"

"Yes, Jacob, I do."

He opened his hand, and there sat a ring box. He asked me to marry him.

In my mind, I was thinking, *I love him but am I in love with him?* Before I knew it, I heard my mouth saying, "Yes!"

He grabbed me and kissed me so passionately, and it felt real to me. We slow hiked back to the car after he made sure social media was on point with our life. Good grief, I hadn't even told my momma yet. By the time I got to my phone it was blowing up! Goodness, was I ready to answer all of the questions?

We got back to my apartment, and I told him I was exhausted.

"I thought we would make love tonight and spend the night together,"

I looked down at my hand, and I thought crap. I need to do something here.

So I said, "I'm sorry baby. Let me run us a bath, and we will relax in the jetted tub and order in some food."

"Perfect and guess what night it is? Scandal night."

That got me pumped up, and I ran us a bath, and we soaked and laughed and talked. It was nice. He wanted some ribs, and I wanted Chinese food.

"Here we go," he said, laughing.

Fortunately, there was a Smoking Ribs next door to Mr. Chi's. I knew the delivery guy, so he hooked us up and stopped and got Jacob a beer to go with his ribs. By the time the food arrived, we were planted in front of the TV watching last week's episode of Scandal. Jacob set up the coffee table like a picnic, and we sat on the floor and chilled out the rest of the night.

I was so tired after we ate and watched the show. He carried me to the bedroom and began to do his thing. I participated, but my heart was not in it. Afterwards, we went to sleep. I had an early case the next morning, so I left before he got up. Yes, this lawyer married a blue-collar worker, but he was a hardworking man and brought home all his money every week.

We married and began a family. Since I was an only child, I thought okay maybe one kid, and then I could continue on my five-year plan and still start my own practice. What do you know? I got pregnant, and boom twins. Wow! They were two beautiful baby boys. There are no twins in my family, but clearly, there is some in his that I did not know about. I did not understand why the doctor did not hear these two heartbeats. Whatever, thank God I have the money to purchase more baby stuff.

Within one year, I was pregnant again with twins, this time, girls. Okay, this works for me, tie me up, burn me up, catch those tubes on fire, do something doctor I do not want any more kids. I am already seeing some changes in Jacob, and for some reason, I feel like we are not going to be together much longer. The doctor had the nerve to ask me, what if I get married again. Dude, I have four kids to raise, I don't think I am going to be a hot commodity anytime soon.

I got my tubes tied during the delivery of the girls. The boys were growing like little weeds, cute as they could be. My little girls had the biggest chunkiest thighs and deepest dimples you ever wanted to see. My sweet little family. I ended up starting my practice and putting the kids in daycare because Jacob seemed to come up missing so much that I couldn't depend on him for jack.

We are celebrating our fourteenth anniversary, and this guy has only been around for seven out of the fourteen and not even consecutively.

My mom said, "You act like you don't care that he is not here to help you."

"I don't care momma, if you knew how much pain, I have suffered from men since I turned sixteen you would understand my reactions."

My heart is numb to the thoughts of real love and someone being faithful to their vows and showing their love. My sons were so sweet to me I guess because they saw how horrible their dad treated me. The girls longed for him and cried for him every night and had an attitude with me because he wasn't at home every night. How in the hell did this become my fault is what I could not understand?

The oldest twin Cody tried so hard to be the man of the home, and I felt so guilty that he had to take on that role. The rest of the kids respected him as the leader of the group. Cody could just feel in the atmosphere when things were wrong with me. My son would send up a note up at work by the guard to tell me how proud he was of me and thankful that I was his mother. Then one day, I went home early, and Cody was just looking and acting strangely.

"Honey are you okay?"

"Sure, momma. Don't worry about anything I'm good." I have never had a problem with him ever before, so I just thought he was having a rough day.

"Honey, you know I am here for you."

"I know Ma." He called Collin and the girls to come down for dinner.

Crap, I had forgotten to pick up something, but Cody had cooked us some fried chicken, macaroni and cheese, broccoli, and rolls. We also had my personal favorite, lemon pound cake. That was odd, but okay, I totally appreciated this man/son of mine. He told the girls to clean up the kitchen, and boy did they start in on him.

He yelled, "Stormy and Summer clean the kitchen, now! Collin, sweep and mop the floor. Get that homework done and bring it to me so I can look it over.

"Cody, I can look it over honey, you look like you might need to lay down."

"Momma, you do everything for us. I have watched you deal with this sperm donor."

"Cody, he is still your father."

"Sorry, Momma, I was using my inside voice." He laughed.

Cody looked at me again and said, "I love you very much mom, and I am so proud of you. You did not allow bad choices in men to stop you from achieving your goals and being successful."

"Thank you so much, son. No one has ever actually said anything to me like that and I believed it with my entire being. I love you and thank you for all you do with these kids; I honestly could not do anything without you. You have been my rock even though you are my son. You graduated early because you put the work in and now you are headed off to college in the fall. That is amazing to me. I think the rest of the kids work so hard because you have set such a great example. Once the girls get their attitude in check, they can hang the moon. Collin will probably work for NASA or something." I laughed. "Go take a break Cody, and I will take care of the homework check tonight. Okay?"

"Okay, love you, momma."

Once Cody left the room, Collin came in and said, "Momma, let's take a walk for a minute."

"Cool." So we took off walking.

"What's going on, baby?"

"Something is happening to Cody. He is so sad lately, and he seems depressed."

"I don't see that Collin."

"Momma, trust me on this; he is my twin, and something is off. Did you know that he has been working so hard with the girls so that that we can all graduate at the same time? He's even been taking us to colleges to look at."

"No, Collin, I did not know about the colleges."

"He acts like he just wants us to get out of here and get on with our lives. Did you know the girls are not cheerleading this year because he told them they will pick up their twelfth-grade math classes after school?"

"What! I asked the girls if they were cheering and they said they wanted to get a job or take a drama class at the theater on the corner. What do you think is happening, Collin?"

"Not sure momma, but I know you are busy, and we are old enough to take care of ourselves, which gives you an opportunity not to helicopter us to death like you used to. Just watch him, momma, I feel something.

"Thank you so much, Collin, for sharing this with me and thank you for being my son."

By the time we got home, Collin immediately started sweeping and mopping the floor. Cody was calling for him to make sure that the task was done and calling for the girls to come to the den with completed homework. I actually started to watch the events in the home instead of leaving the daily ins and outs to Cody.

Jacob decided to make an appearance today and said that he would stay the rest of the week. Hmmm, why has Mr. Invisible shown up? When I look back on the man he was when I met him, to the dude he is now, I wondered what in the world was wrong with me marrying him so quickly? I soon came to understand that I was not in love with him at all and the love I had for him was similar to the love of a friend. Then the babies started rolling in.

I honestly did not know that much about his family after all of these years. Our kids were one year or two years from graduating. One son has taken over the role of man of the home and shame on me for allowing him to walk in power in that position. This came from my own insecurities and longing to have someone love me enough to just take their position in the home. My poor son. Shame on me for allowing the loneliness and feelings of not being good enough to take control over my judgment and lack of understanding of what I was doing to this smart, bright and ambitious young man.

Jacob came in and decided that he was going to try to be a dad. These kids will not respond to him because of Cody. I knew that would happen. I asked Jacob, "How long would his little visit be this time?

"Oh, Sincere, I am home to stay."

"Mighty funny you are coming back now after these kids are practically out of the house. What do you really want Jacob?"

"I miss my family," he said.

"You have been gone off and on for seventeen years now. Cody worked so hard to graduate early so that he could be available to help me with his siblings. I tried to get him to go away to college, but he chose to work during the day while the kids are at school and then he would be off by the time they got out of school. Collin is in his senior year with scholarships to every IT school on the planet. He has a 4.0 GPA and is totally into his craft. Stormy and Summer will be graduating with Collin with honors. Stormy is a math and science genius and wants to be an engineer. She has had four offers from some very prestigious universities, and Summer is the creative out of the bunch. She is a liberal arts major. She is an actress, singer, dancer and art history type of child. A school in New York has offered her a full ride, and it just happened to be the only college that she has ever wanted to attend. Jacob, I do not want your presence to come in here and change the dynamics of this house".

"Sincere, who do you think you are? I am their Father, and I am coming home. They need a father!"

"Jacob, Cody has been their father, and they respect and honor him as the male leader of this home."

"He is a child Sincere! That is what's wrong with you women; you are too weak to take care of your own business."

At that point, Cody came into the room and said,"Look, man, we do not need you here right now. You have not stepped foot in this house for four straight years. No calls, no visits, no money, no nothing; Momma has been doing it all by herself. I just was trying to help my mother who was trying to take care of us, even though she was abandoned by the man that she thought would be here. The difference between you and me man is that I will not leave her. I am her son and her son alone."

Before I knew it, Jacob attempted to attack Cody and told him to stay in a child's place.

"Okay man, momma, I'm going out I'll be back soon."

The girls came flying down the stairs screaming for Cody to come back. He kept walking, and they looked at me as if they were trying to tell me something with those big eyes. I could feel something was wrong, and the girls went upstairs. I jumped in the car and looked back at the house. Collin was in the bedroom window pointing for me to go left. I did and just drove slowly until I saw Cody with some other boys. They were just whooping and hollering. Then my heart dropped, and I saw Cody put on some kind of jacket. It was a gang jacket. What the hell. No!!! I silently screamed. I camped out there for a little while, and I watched the drug deals go down. Cody smacked a woman for not having all of the money. I couldn't breathe. Then the worst thing in the world happened.

Jacob came to the corner with the same Jacket on and everyone kind of jumped to attention. Jacob was the leader and pulled my son into this nonsense. Cody was living a double life, and Jacob was living his trifling life.

I went home and sat on the deck looking into space. Cody came home about two hours later. I think I was still seated in the same spot with my purse on my shoulder and my jacket and heels were still on.

He was calling for me.

"I'm on the deck, Cody."

"Hey lady, why do you still have your stuff on? You should be relaxing."

I just hugged him as tight as I could, and he just laid into my warm embrace. I silently prayed a prayer of comfort and release from the habits and stereotypes of the world.

Collin came downstairs, hugged his brother and said, "Man, I need help on this math problem."

"Don't sweat it, bro. I will be there in a sec."

Then the girls came down, one wanted an idea for a monologue, and one wanted a science question answered.

"Yo! Didn't you guys learn anything at school today? Dang, I'm coming. It's getting late make sure everything else you need to do for tomorrow is done. We all have to be out by 6:30 in the morning. Okay?"

"Now, what teenagers listen to another teenager and does what they are told? I am blessed!"

Cody took my shoes off, took my jacket off and put my purse in the chair. He left and came back with a glass of wine as big as my head. I laughed to myself. He brought my phone, put my jazz on and my earbuds in my ears. I just broke down in tears when he kissed my forehead, and I heard him tell everyone to bring their stuff to the den. Jacob did not come back that night, nor the next night.

It was the second of June, Graduation Day. I had three children graduating with honors, and I was so proud of them. Even Harland's parents came to the graduation with four big fat envelopes. The only thing that my kids knew about Harland was that he hurt me down in my soul, left me broken and disappointed. But God blessed me to keep moving in spite of my pain. God placed their father there to help me heal and give me my beautiful babies.

Collin was the Valedictorian and Summer and Stormy were also on the stage. It was one of the proudest days in my life. After all of the speeches, the Principle of the school asked all four of my children to come to the stage. He complimented Cody for his extreme dedication to his brother and sisters and how because of it the twins were promoted to seniors a year in advance.

He explained how Cody came to him and said, "It is imperative that my brothers and sisters graduate together."

"I gave him a list of requirements and a brother that is only four minutes older than our Valedictorian put these kids into extreme action. I have never seen anything like this in my many years as a principle or in my life as a man. I understand that this is not his graduating class, but I wanted you, young men and women to see the truth about being a youth of honor and determination. His love was not about himself it was geared toward his siblings and his loving mother. People may say where was she, but the thing is she was right there the entire time. She was at every event, parent-teacher conference, and science fair. She was here and was a great example for her children, so this is not taking anything away from Ms. Sincere, this is just to show you all that you have greatness inside of you, and there is someone out there that wants it, craves it, needs it. As you move forward into your life of adulthood, think about this child that took on the role of a man to help his family."

As all of the students went across the stage, I was brought to tears of joy that I now had four high school graduates in the house with me for the summer. We all went out to dinner, even my mother and so called father came. Jacob managed to sober up and come also. It was a beautiful day.

I took off two weeks of work to take the kids to the beach so that they could relax from their years of hard work and dedication. We got back home on a Wednesday. That day I was calling for Cody because I had not seen him in about six hours. I thought he must have been super tired. All of the sudden Collin was screaming for me. I sprinted up the stairs and burst through the door. There he was, laying there lifeless, my son, the head of this house, my great helper in life. I was screaming at the top of my lungs. Collin was trying to hold me.

He kept saying "Don't keep shaking him momma, he is gone."

"Cody! No! What happened to him? Collin, what happened to him?

Through the tears falling from Collin's big brown eyes, he said, "He left a note, momma."

I grabbed it and tried to read it, but I couldn't get the words out for crying, "Why baby, why!!!"

"Momma,do you want me to read this to you?"

I screamed, "We need to call 911!"

"They are on the way."

Why was he so calm, I couldn't understand this at all? I lay down beside my dead son and held him so close.

"Momma, are you ready?" Collin asked.

"Yes."

Dear Momma,

Let me start by saying you are the best momma any of us could have. You were my light through the darkness of my soul. Momma, I never wanted you to worry about anything because of your great loss throughout your life. Your mother shared some of the darkness of your days as a child and an adult. She said that you have never really known love not even from her actually. She told me all of these things my first year of high school so I vowed to myself that I would take care *of you and be here for my siblings so that they will never feel the void of not having a man in their life during their formative years. Momma, this is not your fault or anyone's fault, it is my own weakness that I have had to hide for so many years. I made sure that the girls were not here at all, and it would please me greatly if you would tell them that I died of natural causes. That way they will not feel abandoned by someone they can't even curse out for leaving. You know them two are up for a battle anytime. Lol. What they will remember is that their big brother loved them very much. Collin being the part of me and I a part of him has known of my sickness for a long time. It's because of him that I was able to maintain this long. He did not want you to be alone and sad without me. Momma, I have full-blown AIDS. I have not taken anything from the moment I found out last year. I don't think that it was supposed to be this way, but God kept me healthy enough to keep my mind and body image up until I could get these kids graduated and into college. I know this was probably the wrong way to see Jesus, but it was the right way for me not to bring embarrassment to my family. Momma, I have been in a gang, and I was raped by the members for initiation and later came to find that one of the leaders was infected with the disease, and no one knew until he died recently. I went to the doctor and paid cash for the visit so you would not get the bill. I was full blown, and they only gave me a small amount of time to live. I am so sorry, momma. Burn this letter so that the girls will never ever see this information. Those girls are going to make you proud. They referenced you often as a soldier and woman of God. I loved that you are such an excellent example for them, to women, and for us as a whole. Now Collin knows everything, and he has been a huge part of me staying as healthy as possible with his research of various things to take naturally to help me feel better until this glorious day arrived. He will help you and the girls and you all will be perfect. God knows my heart, and I just pray that He has mercy on my actions.*

I wrote a second letter for each of the girls and Collin has his message in the red computer book on his shelf.

You are a queen mom, and the right man will come for you, and you will never have to worry about him leaving you or hurting you in any way. Just believe that you are worthy of this blessing. If God lets me in because of my love for my family and my love for him, I will send him to you. Just look for the man that says Sincere, I don't want anything from you but you to trust me and let me love you. God will take care of us both. I will take care of the rest. He will look at the kids as his own, and you will be able to tell it's real. It will be a feeling that you have never felt before in your entire life. I love you mom, and I will always be here in your heart. See ya.

By the time the paramedics got there, they were not able to do anything but put him in the body bag and take him away.

Cody wanted to be cremated. Whenever the kids bought their first home, and it looked like they were going to keep it, he wanted to be in the soil with their first planted tree. This way he would be with each of them, and they knew that he was there, and he could meet his nieces and nephews in due time.

My entire life has been filled with loss love and disappointment by men that professed they loved me and left me for no reason. But God blessed me with a son, a man that took responsibility for his family, began a healing process in my heart that helped me more than I have words to express. He was there for seventeen years of my life and a leader in our home since the ninth grade. He never got in trouble at school or at home. He lived the silent screams of a double life that he was too embarrassed to share with anyone. He was so embarrassed that he did what he thought would be the best route to go for all of us. We could have worked it out with God's help I know we could have, but he was a man of decision and decisiveness. He loved me enough not to leave me alone with what could have been some crazy twin girls and a quiet techie boy that could have been some kind of crazy mass murderer because of how quiet he was in the house. But he chose to take his position as a man and make everyone a high school graduate and on the lists of many colleges with so many scholarships just waiting to be given to them. He set a foundation and a standard of love and respect, and I know they will complete the tasks that he has laid before them. I could say that I was abandoned again, but I can honestly say this was a silent scream of love.

SILENCE OF LONGING

Longing Creates Toxic Habits.

The sound of my alarm at 4am was like death to my soul, but I was on a mission. I rolled off my bed and got on my knees to give thanks for so many blessings that I had and asked God to let me be a blessing to someone else today. I jump up and could smell the aroma of this new coffee I bought yesterday. It is the Noble King coffee. My neighbor's pastor thought why not get into the coffee business since he utilizes coffee shops all of the time. I totally support him, so she brought my bag of dark roast last night and put it on my counter. It smells delicious; I can barely finish brushing my teeth. I crack myself up the way I love coffee.

Okay, Sage, it's 4:30 already, time to get those gym clothes on and go meet these other crazy 5am boot camp people. I am about to be fifty years old, and I need to make sure I keep everything where it is supposed to be at this age. I decided to commit to a boot camp for the remainder of the year and then before I am fifty I will take on a triathlon. The class begins with some nice stretching and getting limber to prepare the body for the next forty-five minutes of a beat down. It was horrible; we jumped with a big black ball that felt like iron was in it. I was proud I did not quit.

As I was getting ready to leave, I looked at my classmate Don and said, "We are paying him to do this to us. You know that right?"

He laughed and said, "I know right!"

Fortunately, the gym was a good two blocks from my brownstone, so I did not have to pull my car out of its space. That is a plus.

The bellman greeted me, "Good morning Ms. Harris."

"Sam, you can call me Sage."

"It has taken you three years to call me Sam so give me a minute," he smiled.

"Yes, Sir, I replied."

Sam was a nice man, but there was sadness behind his smile that resembled the sadness I feel sometimes.

My life was full, and I should be happy inside and out, but I am not. I feel as though nothing I do is ever enough. I live in the heart of Manhattan in a beautiful brownstone, I work in corporate America, I make over seven figures, and it grows every year. I love my job; I am a Vice President of a Finance Company. We are doing extremely well this year, so I can't complain in that department. Although it is a corporate environment, we treat everyone with the utmost respect and gratitude for a job well done. I work late a few times a month so that I can spend time with our night staff. We have so many housekeepers and night auditors that would never have the opportunity to meet us if we did not make an effort to get to know them. It is just respectful and thank goodness the President of the company has the same thoughts about maintaining a healthy workplace culture as I do.

So again, I am forty-nine years old, and I have no children, ex-husband or current husband. Hell, I don't even have a boyfriend. What a joke to me. My dear friend Beth told me just to be patient, maybe my husband is going through some things, and he is trying to get his stuff together before he comes into my life. Beth has an amazing husband and three great kids. They are my godchildren, so in a way, I kind of have children because they have no problem calling Auntie Sage to ask if I can pick them up and buy them stuff with the black card. Ha! Love those little rascals.

At work and in this community, I am the bright, bubbly, lovely smiling, help anyone, love everyone, Sage. My problem comes when I go home alone. It's not that I don't meet men, it's just I haven't met anyone that holds my interest for an extended period of time. It can be so wonderful, but if something changes in communication or if they are just not there when I really need them, I seem just to revert backward to he has probably lost interest in me. Does this mean something is wrong with me?

After I fixed me a light snack before bed, I decided to defy my boot camp rule of no drinking during the eight-week period of training. I proceeded to fix me a double Jack and Coke to go along with my sweet fruit bowl. I sat on my window sofa with the window open. I could hear the jazz band play at the club across the street. It was nice, and I didn't have to pay for a twenty dollar drink that I could fix at home. As I sat there, I realized I had never been to that club, but part of me didn't want to go alone or with just anyone. I wanted to go with that someone. Whoever and wherever he may be.

Sitting in that window couch after dark is my entertainment. There are a few shows that I like to look at but for the most part in the evening is me and my friend Jack. When I looked up, I had gotten up at least three times and refilled my empty glass. As I dragged myself to my room, the thought of my bed bothered me tonight. Why do I have a California King just for me? I don't need it but it sure is comfortable, and maybe one day someone will be here with me.

The sun was piercing through my window letting me know that it was the weekend. My head hurts, I need coffee! What should I do today? Once I get my life together, I will walk the town and see what is new. I got my coffee and made a note to have Liz to get me another bag of the coffee or tell me how to order it for myself. The next thing I knew, I was sitting in the sauna in my shower sobbing my eyes out.

I cried out to God asking him why was I so lonely? Please tell me what to do. You said you would give us the desires of our hearts. My desire is to be a wife and belong to one man that wants a wife to love. No games, cheating, mental abuse none of that crap. Seen it, felt it, didn't like it, don't want it. Something real is what my heart craves.

Some days I am overly obsessive. The only consistent relationship I have at night is with a bottle of Jack and a depression pill. Wait they are not supposed to go together but some nights are unbearable, and I cry in my sleep. I take a pill to make sure I don't wake up during the night. What a pathetic life. It could be worse, though.

The funny thing to me is that my friends that are married absolutely hate it and think that I am living the life. I want everything they despise about marriage like letting someone else know where you are. The big one they complain about is answering the question, what's for dinner, and not wanting to have sex every day.

My friend Liz says, "Sage, you want it so bad because you never had it."

Beth says, "God is molding him and making him just for you so be patient." Sometimes I think if I hear that one more time I might choke.

Let me get out of this house! What can I do today to make a difference was my mission? A new bookstore had opened up, and it looked like it was a locally owned little store. I popped in, and it had a coffee shop/bar in the back. It had an upstairs section. I looked on the message board, and they have open mic nights for spoken word and book groups. Good grief this is awesome. It looks like I may get a life through this bookstore. I dabble in poetry a little and have some really great pieces that I would like to share. I picked up a couple of books and asked the cashier who the owner was and how long had the store been open?

She said, "Mr. King is the owner. Would you like to meet him? He is really sweet and likes to meet all of his new customers."

I liked that because that is how I treat my employees. Immediately I thought, he is probably an old guy and married for fifty years. Why do I do that? Then I thought sure, I would like to meet him. My mission today was to help someone, so maybe I could help him if he needs it. Being a local owner is hard work up here. While I was waiting, I saw some kids sitting in a circle, and a lady was about to read a story. I sat down in the circle too. The kids looked at me like okay she is a big kid too, so they leaned into me. The story was good. It was "The Giving Tree." I loved that book as a kid.

I noticed an extremely tall good looking man staring at me during the story, but those kids were sitting on my lap, and I turned into a parent. It was cool, though. When the story was over the kids gave the storyteller and me a hug. I told the cashier if Mr. King was busy I would totally be back next weekend for the spoken word event, and maybe I could meet him then.

She asked, "Ms. what is your name?"

"I'm sorry Katie, I am Sage Harris."

Katie said, "can you hold on for a minute. He will be right down."

"That's fine," I replied.

It felt so good in the store I wasn't ready to leave. They must have put on a fresh pot of coffee because the room was illuminated with a robust smell of coffee beans. Yummy! My brain yelled to my stomach. My stomach pushed me to the coffee shop in the back, and I ordered a large coffee with a hint of French Vanilla. Whoa! It was Mr. Handsome that kept staring at me in the bookstore. He looked just like my coffee, tall, dark and sweet.

He said, "That will be four dollars, ma'am."

At that moment a kid came and tugged at my shirt. "I want a book."

"Where is your mommy, sweetie?"

"She said she didn't have money for the book."

"Oh okay, let me talk to her first and see if it is okay for me to buy it."

"I told her that I was going to ask you, and she said okay."

Well, about two seconds later two more kids asked me to buy them a book. Goodness!

So I paid Mr. Handsome for my coffee and followed these children to the parents. They looked so disgusted with life. I introduced myself to them collectively and asked them if they would mind if I treated their children to some books. A light came into their eyes, so that alone told me, lady, please and thank you.

One of them said, "we can't let you do that," but I insisted, and they all agreed. We gathered up all the kids, and I followed them as they held on to the items that they wanted. There were eight children, and they were saying can I have this, can I have that?

"Each of you can have five things, okay."

Their eyes were as big as the sun as they followed behind me like my little ducklings. We waddled up to Katie, the cashier, and each child put their items on the counter. Katie handed them their individual bags. The bill came up to one thousand six hundred dollars, and they were amazed.

We went back to the parents, and I said, "Hopefully, something in these bags will hold their attention long enough so you can have a break today."

They laughed. What I did notice was that each of those kids bought their mother a gift. One child bought a cup with "Real Mommies Read to Their Kids," one had a nice journal and pen set, another one bought a Cosmopolitan magazine and a Parenting Crafting magazine. Another kid bought her mom a bag of coffee with a cup. All of them loved their mommies so! I was happy to be apart of the looks on the parents' faces when the kids presented their gifts to their moms first before showing them what they bought for themselves. That let me know that they are loved and are doing a great job as parents.

I felt a tear rolled down my face. I am not used to this kind of love from anyone. I was alone in the world, no parents, no kids, no one just me. The ladies got up and individually gave me a hug. They wrote their phone numbers down and said if I ever wanted to get together for coffee, please give them a call. That was so sweet.

When I turned around Mr. Handsome was right there and told me that he wanted to give me a fresh cup of coffee. Somewhere along the way, I sat my cup down to help one of the kids pull down a book.

"Wow, that was so sweet and kind," he said. "No, you are sweet and kind. I saw what you did for those kids."

"The smile on all of their faces was worth so much more than what I spent, so it was a beautiful day. Thanks again sir for the coffee."

"Oh, what's your name?" I asked?

"Kent."

"Nice to meet you, Kent. My name is Sage."

I grabbed my little bag that Katie was holding for me and said, "Katie, I have been here for a long time, I will catch up with Mr. King another day."

She looked confused but said, "Okay, bye Sage."

Doing things for someone else makes me feel like I am doing something for the greater good of others. It was small to me but meant the world to those ladies, and I am thankful to have the means to do so.

By the time I got home, I was hungry. I looked at the clock. I had been at that bookstore for four hours. The spirit of the store made me feel good from the inside out. Not sure that I have ever felt that way about a retail shop. I fixed me some stir fry and fruit for lunch and plopped down in front of the TV. It was beautiful outside, but for some reason, I was exhausted.

Yay! A Tyler Perry movie marathon was on so let the fun begin. After the first movie Good Deeds, my mind started to go haywire thinking about how I have to keep up this business persona in public. If I had my way, I would own a yoga studio, sell organic clothes, oils and organize spa retreats to Bali and Costa Rica for women that need a break. Women that need to become one with themselves so they can be the best at everything they do. If they could come up with half of the funds just to show effort, I would pay the rest. My heart says one thing, but my occupation doesn't match my inner heart. It's cool though because I love what I do, and I'm good at it.

Here it comes! I need a drink. I waited for a commercial and marched into the kitchen and got a new bottle of Jack, Coke, a bowl of ice and put it on a tray and sat it on the coffee table. It was only 5pm, and I had already had three drinks and some snacks. After the fourth movie, I was going stir crazy, and I felt depression set in for real.

I jumped up and went to the bathroom and turned on the shower and all of the shower heads so I could be hit in every direction so I could not hear myself cry. Then I turned on the sauna and just sat on the bench and went into the darkest place of loneliness. Would anyone miss me if I just ended my life right now? No, they wouldn't. I have no one in my life that loves me the way I want to be loved. If I were to get it, would I recognize it? Probably not; My heart has been destroyed by love or the pretense of love from a man. I have been used and mentally abused by Mr. No Good more times than I care to acknowledge.

My phone started ringing back to back, so I jump out of the sauna and grab it in a panic. It was one of the kids from the bookstore, and she said Katie at the bookstore gave her my phone number.

"I need help," she said. Aries was a sweet little twelve year old that helped me with the smaller kids today.

I asked her how I could help her.

She said, "Can you meet me at the diner by the bookstore?

"Sure, where is your momma?"

"She is at home with my brothers and sisters. She knows I am at the bookstore."

"Okay, give me twenty minutes I just got out of the shower."

I did not know what I was going to walk into or what to expect from a twelve-year-old girl that looks sixteen. I put on some jeans and a shirt and grabbed a wrap to wrap my hair up. Pretty much sprinted to the diner. There she was sitting all alone, and her eyes were so sad. I put on my happy face and greeted her with a hug. Aries hugged me so tightly and said thanks for coming Ms. Sage.

"Are you hungry Aries or would you like a dessert?"

"Coke and dessert would be cool." We both ordered strawberry shortcake and a Coke.

"What's wrong baby girl?"

"Let's just talk about something else first," she said.

"That was so wonderful what you did for us kids at the bookstore. You will never really know how you made my momma feel today. She had promised my brothers and sisters that she was going to buy those books and games for them for months, but she just couldn't get it together in the money part of our lives." She shared.

"Aries, she has something that I will never have so she gave me a great gift today by allowing me to be a blessing to the kids. Honestly, my money department is on point, but I don't have any family or anyone so either side can be stressful."

"Ms. Sage, how old are you anyway."

"Girl, don't go asking me my age now!" We both started laughing. "I said I will be forty-nine in two weeks."

"Really! I thought you were like in your twenties or something."

"Aries, you can say that to me anytime."

We finished our desserts and got a refill on our Cokes.

"Are you ready to talk now?"

She took a deep breath, "Okay here is the deal. I was messing around with this dude."

"Wait, messing around how?"

"He was teaching me how to kiss and stuff, and he started touching me down there, but that was the first time. Then I began to want to see him more and learn some more stuff because I liked how it made me feel on the inside. He was all about me seems like, he looked at me and when we were together, he was just with me. Unlike those married losers my mom dates. I had to grow up fast and help her raise these kids. All of us got different daddies, and none of them do anything for us except June's father. He is kind of cool. He is married, but he always pays child support in cash and brings us groceries and all of us gifts when he brings her gifts. So that is great!"

"Groceries you guys don't have groceries daily?"

"No Sage we do not. We eat a lot of ramen noodles, rice, and bologna."

I was crying on the inside and called myself a rich bitch because I did not even know what a ramen noodle was or what it was made out of! I hate myself right now.

"Okay, back to the dude Aries."

"His name is Rodney. He makes me feel so wanted, and he is so funny. The last time we hung out, I let him do it to me."

"Do it to you?"

"You know we had sex."

My heart dropped. My first question was, "Have you talked to him since then?"

"Everyday, I love him so much, but I'm only twelve right now. I will be thirteen tomorrow."

"How old is he Aries?"

"He just turned fifteen last week."

"When did this happen, Aries?"

"Last month for the first time but we do it all the time, and I like it. No kids are screaming, no momma, just us, and he fixes me food and brings it to me, and we watch TV together. He will even watch stuff I like when the game is on. He loves me."

I thought to myself he has had a great example in his home. He does love her.

"Do you need me to talk to your mom with you about birth control or something?"

"No need I have not had a period in a month."

"Aries, when did you start your period?"

"I started when I was eleven years old."

That would explain that little body that she has going on. Goodness! A child I just met is putting this huge secret in my hands, head, and heart.

"Would you like me to go with you to tell your momma?"

"Yes, and I would like you to take this kid when I have it."

Whoa there sister, I thought. What the heck! I'm almost fifty this kid will be eighteen, and I will be nearly seventy years old. I took a sip of my Coke and thought, Oh Jack where are you?

Aries just kept her eyes locked on mine.

"Let's tell your momma first and then see what her thoughts are about the kid."

"Ms. Sage, you look like I just hit you with a truck. We can wait until next weekend. She takes us to the bookstore every Saturday since it opened."

"Bless you girl for picking up on my heart rhythm speeding up to heart attack mode."

She hugged me and said, "Thanks for listening."

"Anytime, lock my number in your cell phone just in case you need me for anything."

I went back home and grabbed my remote to cut on the jazz music station. Then I remembered it was jazz night at the club across the street, so me and my Gentleman Jack got set up on the window couch and I used a huge wine glass for this drink, and I had some great cheese and crackers. The jazz started immediately.

The moon seemed to find its way through the clouds to shine right down on me tonight. I drank that glass so fast it made my head immediately spin. Then I realized I had not even put the Coke in the glass. I sat there listening to the music and being lost in my loneliness. All of a sudden I felt the tears come down my face, but these tears were different. Is it possible that my lonely days and nights could be filled with the laughter of a beautiful baby girl or boy? Usually, I would roll myself to the bed after drinking so much in the course of a day, but this time, I did not even make it to the bed. I reached up and grabbed a pillow from the bed and slept on the floor.

My loneliness consumes me to the point that I need to numb myself every night to take the place of love and oneness with another person. If I blank out, I can't feel anything but the spinning of the room when I close my eyes. I lay on the floor all night without sleep or rest. The morning came so quickly. I sat up on the floor and looked up to God to help me and this sickness that has consumed my life. Depression is a quiet killer of self-worth and self-love in which I seemed to have neither.

Show me what to do with myself and come out of this alcoholic, lonely state of mind. Help me and guide me, please. One thing I do know about life is God will help you out of all of your troubles. I thanked Him for all that I had and asked him to let me do something to help someone today that is burdened.

It is 6am on Sunday morning, and my phone is ringing. I jump up to get the phone, and it's Aries. She is crying her eyes out, and I am trying to stay calm and ask questions.

"Aries, I can't understand you so take it easy and tell me where you are I will come to you."

"I'm at home," she sobbed.

"My mom saw the pregnancy papers in my drawer, and she was beating me. I ran to the bathroom and locked the door."

"Aries do you want me to come or do you want me to call the police."

"She said she would calm down in a minute. At least momma didn't hit me in the stomach. I know that it is just fear because she can barely take care of us and now a baby."

The phone went dead. Goodness! I sat there on the floor, and I prayed if you let her call me back, I will go to AA and see a therapist for help. Please, I will take care of her if you can help me take care of me. The prayer was prayed, and the phone rang again about an hour later. It was the longest hour of my life.

"Aries!!"

"No, it is her mother, Sandra."

"Hello, Ms. Sandra."

There was silence on the phone.

"Hello?" I asked again.

"Sage, my daughter just told me that she had asked you to take this baby if she has it. Did you agree to this?"

"I did not; I just need a little more time to think about it."

Sandra continued, "Sage, I have four kids already all under the age of thirteen. I can barely clothe and feed them. I can't handle another mouth to feed. If you do not take this kid, then she will have to go to my aunts, give birth to the child, and give it up for adoption. That is all that I know to do."

I asked Sandra if I could come over later and bring lunch after church. She said sure. I hung up the phone and went to brush my teeth and wash my face to make sure that I was awake. As I watched myself in the mirror, I noticed that I did look young and that I really was an attractive woman. I dropped my shirt and bared myself and thought, you have the body of a thirty year old, and you have a beautiful soul. Why don't you love yourself, Sage? You have created this deep depression and feeling of unworthiness. I got in the shower, but I did not cry. Got out and put on some running clothes and took a three mile run before I got ready for church.

Upon my return home, the bellman said "Happy new beginnings, Ms. Sage."

While I was on the elevator, I was thinking today is my fresh start. I went into the kitchen and looked in my alcohol closet. Dang, I was a straight alcoholic all by myself. I bought four liters of Jack just two weeks ago, and they were all gone. So I grabbed my trash and goodness, there was no food papers just Coke bottles and empty containers of alcohol. I started to cry tears of joy that I do not have to live this life anymore. I will find my happiness in bringing joy to others.

I cleaned out my fridge and emptied the liquor closet. I bagged up some of the wine I had for the bellman and his wife. I had a nice bottle of twenty-fice year old whiskey that a client gave me last year. I put that by the door and finished cleaning up the kitchen.

Okay, time for church. My church was a block away, and I was able to walk there in my heels with no problem. The service was about the beauty of God's grace and how when we open our hearts we can feel the peace that passes all understanding. You know, we hear these things over and over, but today it clicked in my heart and soul what that meant to me for my life. I went to the altar for prayer and a prophetess named Sister Laura, whispered so sweetly in my ear that God was about to make all things new in my life, and the love that I seek is already with me.

She said, "Sage there no need to drink another drop or feel unloved ever again. The seeds that you have sown in other people's life are ready for harvest. You will reap a harvest that will be the exact desire of your heart. Trust God and believe His word."

She hugged me so sweetly and patted my face and said, "Mark the words of the Lord. God is calling you."

I knew it was God because she did not have a clue about my self-destructive behaviors.

It was about 1pm. I pre-ordered a huge dinner from the deli and some food for the week for Sandra and the kids. The deli was in their area, so I went home jumped in my car and took off to their home Sandra had texted me the address during church. I asked the deli driver to deliver the food by 2pm. We got there at the same time. Perfect.

I knocked on the door, and the little ones said, "Hey Lady! Did you bring us something?"

"I sure did."

I had the deli attendant pick up some gift cards to the toy store from the connecting Walgreens.

"Where is your mom?"

"Mommy!"

Sandra came around the corner with such sadness in her eyes. I felt my soul drop to the ground. I opened my arms and embraced her with all the love and compassion that I had in me. She lay there and wept.

The driver said, "Ladies, where would you like the food?"

"Oh my goodness, I thought you were going to grab some burgers or something," Sandra exclaimed!

"Girl, I'm hungry. We are going to eat some good stuff and a bunch of it," I said, laughing.

This deli was exquisite in service; not only will they deliver the food but will set the table up in a family style buffet. He brought paper products all types of beverages and desserts. I have one special dessert for Aries, strawberry shortcake with extra strawberries and whipped cream and a Coke with a lot of ice.

Sandra smiled, "Thank you, sir." Assuming he was done placing the food on the table.

"I have one or two more trips to make, and then I will be done."

"What else is he bringing?"

"I just picked up a few items to bring you for a couple of weeks."

"Sage you did not have to do that."

"Will you please accept it? Please let me do this for you and your beautiful children."

Sandra opened up the fridge and freezer and started putting the food away. The cabinets were all empty but not anymore. We called the kids in, and we all sat down and began to eat. She did not have another table for us to sit to eat because the food was on the dining room table. We just sat all over the place, laughed, and talked and then, the discussion came. The kids were sent to go play while the three of us talked.

The little one Jamison said, "I thought you brought us something."

"Sage, no that is enough," Sandra said, eyeing her son.

"I can't return these gift cards, Sandra," I said with puppy dog eyes.

She laughed and said, "thank you so much."

I gave each child a gift card to the toy store and gave Sandra a Visa card with enough on there to buy them all some new outfits.

"Why did you do all of this for us? We just met you yesterday."

"God has blessed me so that I can be a blessing to others.

"Now about Aries, what do you want to do again, Sandra?"

"I want her to leave here and go out of town to my aunts and stay with them until the baby comes and then give it up for adoption. If you don't want to be a mom, that is all I can do; she is thirteen. That is too young for an abortion. What am I supposed to do, just sit here and let her be like me? No, I can't do it!"

"Calm down, I have been praying, and I believe that this is meant for me to raise this baby as my own."

Aries, the sweet adult face had tears in her eyes said, "Thank you because I could never kill my baby. Will you let me see the kid even though it will live with you?"

"Yes, we will work it all out so that as long as you want to be in the baby's life, you are welcome. Just promise me that you all won't give me this gift and then take it away from me."

We all agreed that we would work as a team and have a healthy birth mom and baby. I hugged and kissed everyone. We will choose a good Obgyn doctor for Aries and an attorney to help with the proceedings.

"I don't want to sell the baby, Ms. Sage."

"I want to do everything legally so that we are all clear on what we want for the baby and you," I explained.

On the drive home, all I could think about was all of the possibilities of being a mom and taking care of someone for the rest of my life. I giggled. What a day! I was so thankful to get home tonight. I could tell the house was different. I forgot that the housekeeper was coming today, Sunday because she had some things to do with her family Monday morning. I love her. She is so sweet, she loves what she does, and that is amazing. Amelia is my housekeeper's name, and she left me a note. It said, Sage, I am so proud that you have decided to stop drinking. I was thinking how in the world did she know that? As I continued to read the note, she stated how concerned she had become about me and how many empty bottles she emptied every week. She wanted to leave me some AA information. She must have noticed my liquor cabinet was empty, and the trash was out. That made me happy that she saw my change of life. I took off my clothes, got in the bed, googled newborn, and started reading about how to care for one. Life is changing, and I had a ray of hope in my grasp. All I could do is say thank you, God.

My mind turned to the fact that it was about to be Monday and that 4am boot camp was going to happen after eating strawberry shortcake, Coke and heaven knows how much alcohol. For once in a long time, I went to bed happy and beat the alarm clock up this morning. Instead of walking to class, I did a light jog to try to make up for some of the crap I ate this weekend. I did my workout and left so that I could get ready for work.

We grossed quite a bit over the weekend in revenue, and that was incredible. I looked at my calendar and noticed it was time to visit with second shift and overnighters today. I ordered a special dinner for them and had it all laid out at their lunch time. I ate and chatted with them and asked some questions about work and if they needed anything from upper management. Everyone seemed to be happy which made me euphoric. My goal is to make sure that everyone feels like they are a part of the team and the vision for the company. My housekeeper, at home, works here also. She cleans outside of work, and I make sure she is paid well in both places.

I let them know that whatever food is left over they can feel free to take it home. The caterers brought to-go boxes just in case. "Bye, Ms. Harris," they chimed as I was leaving.

It was about 8pm by the time I got to my neighborhood. Oh yeah, tonight is that spoken word thing at the bookstore so why not go while I am still dressed. I need to be around others while I detox my system.

I walked into the bookstore, and Katie said, "Hello Ms. Sage!"

"Hi, Katie!"

We chatted for a minute, and she said, "Mr. King really wants to meet you tonight. He will be here a little later."

She leaned over and whispered, "He heard what you did for those kids, and I don't think I have ever seen such a twinkle in his eye before."

"Hmmm, girl, it was nothing. I woke up wanting to make someone happy. What time does the show start?"

"You are just in time; everyone is upstairs."

"Will they have something to drink up there?"

"Yes a bar and specialty coffee for those that do not want to sleep at night." We laughed.

I went upstairs and sat with a couple. They were nice. The first poet got up, and he talked about the loneliness in silence and not knowing what to do when the depths of your soul longs for love, peace, and true happiness. I cried because I knew that feeling oh to well. All of the poets were phenomenal, and the last person that came on stage was that guy from the bookstore; Mr. Tall, dark and sweet.

He said, "I want to thank everyone for coming out tonight. I also want to share a thought with you about a special young woman that is in our midst this evening. I will not call her out, but I wrote a poem for her. It's called the Sweetness of Life."

"I saw you from across the room and saw the light in your eyes. My soul longed for you. At that moment, you smiled as the kids played in your hair. My heart wanted you. How freely you gave yourself to those without anything. I knew you. You were me, and I was you. I asked God that night if he would let you think of me and know that I am you, and you are me.

Lord, what can I do to let her know that I have prayed for her my entire life and when we officially meet, that she will feel that she is me, and we are we."

The crowd went crazy, and I blushed from within. Then this handsome man came over to my table and held out his hand and said, "Hello Ms. Sage it is a pleasure to finally meet you officially."

"Kent, you're Mr. King, the owner of the bookstore? Wow! Thank you for the poem it was beautiful."

He said, "Walk with me for a moment." I thought, why not?

We went downstairs and out the door. We walked close to my building and then I heard the jazz music that "Jack" and I usually listen to together. Kent asked me if I had eaten.

"No, actually I have not."

"Would you like to go to the Jazz and Dinner Club?"

This is my man! I heard my heart scream to my head. We had the best time. I found out that we have the same goals and aspirations of life. We want to use our blessings to bless others.

"Where do you live Sage?"

I pointed up to the brownstone across the street and pointed to my door.

"Really? Oh, I am sorry you probably eat here all the time."

"No actually, I never wanted to go until I was with you." That was one of the best nights of my life.

Three months passed and Aries was starting to poke out a little more every day. I decided to invite all the kids and their parents over to my house for dinner and a movie. Everyone got there, and the caterer had everything prepared just in time.

One of Sandra's kids said, "Ms. Sage, do you cook at all?" I burst out laughing.

"I do, but I eat so sparingly that I would rather have someone do it for me, so no one gets sick." Everyone laughed!

As the evening was winding up, Sandra asked if Aries could stay with me for the last month of the pregnancy. I said, "Yes!" without hesitation.

"That way you both can get the nursery together as a team. Plus, I don't want that baby to come, and I have to load up all these kids in the wee hours of the morning."

"I totally understood that fear."

I asked Aries if she was cool with that and she was. She did ask me if it was okay if Rodney could come over and meet me so he would feel good about the decision that she made to give the baby to me; I told her it was no problem.

My relationship with Kent was taking off fast. I needed to let him know that I'd made this obligation to Aries and the baby so he could have the opportunity to bolt if he did not want that type of responsibility in his life. He is about four years younger than me, and he does not have any children so maybe he will be cool with it. Due to some tragedy in my teenage years, I was not going to be able to produce kids anyway.

The next night after work Kent invited me to the bookstore to hang out with him while he did inventory. I drank some coffee, moved some boxes, and helped him count stuff until late in the evening. When we finally finished, we went to the diner next door and had a big fat juicy hamburger.

He said, "I know I shouldn't but do you want to split a strawberry shortcake with me?" I love him!

"Kent where are we in this relationship right now? Do you see us long term?"

"I see us getting married soon if you want me." He replied.

"Good, I want you, but I need to share something with you. I have obligated myself to adopt a baby of a thirteen year old girl."

"Aries, right?"

"Yes, how did you know that?"

"She came to me and told me what was going on in her life. I told her she should find you and talk to you because you seemed like such a sweet woman."

"Well, if you see us as long term that baby will be our baby. Will that work for you?"

"Yes, Sage. I want a child so bad, but I have not met a woman that I felt would be a good mother and wife."

All I could say is my life is complete.

The baby came without complications and Kent, and I had a beautiful wedding.

Once I surrendered to God, He blessed me with a family and real love.

I am grateful.

FAMILY SECRETS

Secrets of the Family Can Destroy the Family

When you have a big family, there is bound to be a secret of some kind that has been swept under that damnable rug of secrets. Will the family secret stop anyone from being who they have been all along? It really depends on the depth of the secret and the character of the person that the lie has affected.

"Eli, did you dry your uniform last night?"

"No, Ma!"

"Well, mister I know you did not because the dryer stopped working."

"Maaaa!! Can you take it to the wash center thing on the corner for me?"

"Eli, it is 5:30 in the morning, I know you did not just ask me if I could do that."

"Ha-ha, you are hearing things. I am going to run down there and dry my uniform."

She smiled so sweetly at me, but her eyes were super sad. I was not sure what was happening, but I had to go.

This wash center stays open twenty-four hours. At first, I thought, who washes their clothes all hours of the night but being in my situation right now, boy am I glad I didn't set the closing hours. I found a dryer and put my uniform inside.

It was the last game of the year, and graduation was in three days. I am so happy to have had parents that made me study and work hard. I have a 4.0 GPA and three scholarships in my hands. A scout for the Falcons has contacted my dad. While I was sitting there waiting, I remembered I am leading the hot topics in Sociology class this morning.

The headline in the paper today was about human trafficking and black market babies. Trying to comprehend the fact that human trafficking is real, made me angry. Someone decides to steal kids and sell them to perverts for money, and that is their purpose in life really! The black market baby situation is just as bad when a woman has a child, and some jerk takes it upon themselves to get the kid and sell it for an unspeakable amount to people who can't have children. I am so glad that my mom did not have to go through any of that crap.

My uniform was dry by the time I got my topics together. As soon as I got back, breakfast was on the table. My dad is usually talking so much about sports, and my opportunities that I can't get a word in. Mom is always saying, let the boy eat Danny. This morning they were both pretty quiet, and it was really weird. Maybe they were all sentimental because I am getting ready to go to school and our breakfast time will be cut short. I asked them if they were okay. They both just looked at me as if I had three heads. I grabbed the plates and took them into the kitchen. My mom followed me and gave me a big hug and kiss and asked if I was leaving now.

"Yes, Ma'am. I have to rehearse for my graduation speech."

"Be careful honey!"

"Bye, dad!" Out the door, I went.

By the time I got to the school my phone was ringing. It was my mom. "Make sure you come home right after the game we need to talk to you."

"Okay, Ma!"

Sociology is my first class with Mr. Garrett. He is a great teacher.

"Eli, you are leading the discussion this morning," he said as I walked in.

I began to tell the class about the trafficking ring that was going right through our city. I explained how unaware we as teenagers are while we are out and about doing everything under the sun. Just as quickly as we can blink our eyes someone can convince us to come with them. The black market for babies is a ridiculous thought to us, but it is happening right in front of us everyday; but because we are so into our own groove of life, we are not paying attention.

Mr. Garrett looked at me and said, "Dang! Eli, this is a heavy topic for 7:30 in the morning."

"You wanted me to keep it relevant, so here it is."

For one moment Mr. Garrett just stared at me to the point that I was like what is going on with the adults in my life this morning.

I got through all the classes, my game, and graduation rehearsal. At home, my momma was cooking dinner. The family had started arriving for the graduation. I have two sisters and four brothers, and I am the youngest, the seventh child. I loved it because I could try anything and if I got stumped one of them knew something about it. They are all older than me. I think I must have been an oops baby. That was cool for me, though.

My dad heard me pull up and come in the back door.

"Eli!", He belted. Come to our room now!"

I was like what is wrong with them? I am doing good in school, why does he sound so mad?

I loved my parent's room. It was the entire length of the house; they had their own wing if you will. There was an office off their bedroom and the closet. It was a cool room. Dad was waiting for me at the door, and my mom was sitting on the couch. She had her arms outstretched to me, "Sit here Eli."

"What's up parental units?"

We watched Coneheads the night before, so they laughed a little bit. Then immediately went back to being so serious. Mom looked at my dad and motioned for him to start talking.

He said in his deep voice, "Eli, you know that we love you so much. You have made us so proud, and it is an honor to be your parents.

"Okay, so whats happening you guys are freaking me out a little."

He said, "Eli, you are not our biological child."

"What?!"

"You are Sharon's son.

"My sister?!"

"Yes, she had you when she was fifteen years old. There was no way she could raise you due to her lifestyle, being wild and crazy, and we could not let her take you to God knows where and something happen to you. We have been being blackmailed by your birth father, and we did not want a scene to occur at your graduation and you not be aware.

"What does he want?"

"He seeks to be a part of your life. He found out about your possibility of playing for the Falcons and now we can't get rid of him. We are not sure of how he even knew this information. By you only being seventeen it has not been televised, per our request. We hired a private investigator and found out that Mr. Garrett, your teacher, is your grandfather. Eli, the only reason we did not tell you sooner is because we wanted to keep you safe from confusion and corrupt behaviors. The man has always known about you and has never once acted like he wanted to spend time with you or get to know you for the wonderful man that you have always been. Dad wanted you to be a great leader one day with the know-how of being a real leader in the home and community."

"Mom looked at the ground and said, all my life I wanted a relationship with my father, but he did not have the mental ability to be consistent with me. He would be there full force for about three months then I would not see him for several years.

She continued, "When dad asked me to marry him, the only thing I said was on one condition, if we have children, you have to take your position as husband, father, leader and provider in the home. Not just in money but in being a provider of your time and effort to each child according to their individual needs. God be the glory he did just that."

Sharon was my hardest child to deal with; she was arrogant and sometimes the face of evil, but I knew for certain that some of our genes were flowing through her. We just had to deal with her where she was in her mind and in her life. In the process, she came home one day and just blurted out, 'I got a baby in here' and pointed to her stomach. Dad looked like his neck was about to burst with veins of anger and emotion. He looked at me and touched my hand and calmly asked Sharon what she wanted to do about it? She said, 'I know this family doesn't believe in abortion, so I won't take you all there. I guess I'll have to have it and see what happens.' I asked who the father was. She said, Ellis Garrett.

We did not even know this boy. We took her to the doctor and did all we could to provide the best pregnancy we could. We made sure she ate the right foods, took her vitamins, exercised and went to education classes on being a new mother.

On that cold September morning, we got a call from Sharon; she had spent the night at Aunt Genna's house. 'Mom!' she screamed, 'It is happening right now!' I woke your dad up, and we quickly got dressed and met them at the hospital. It was the fastest delivery I have ever seen. You came out like a superhero with one arm out, and a bald up fist like you were holding up the power to the people sign. When I saw your eyes, goodness! It was the most beautiful angelic face that I had ever seen. My first grandchild. My soul leaped with joy and laughter from within. Dad looked like a prize rooster. His chest was all poked out, and he said, 'That is a good looking boy right there!'

Sharon held you, but she looked so strange and unsure of everything. I asked her if she needed anything. She said it was probably the meds and not to worry. I had to drag dad from the hospital so he could get some rest because he had a big day at work the next day. He tossed and turned all night long. Finally, he shook me awake around 4am. He said something was wrong with Sharon on yesterday. He said he could feel it. I told him to try to rest, and I held him so that he could sleep for an hour or so before he had to get up. Dad went on to work, and I went to the hospital. When I got there, Ellis, your biological dad was there. He wanted Sharon to sell you to a couple that did not have any kids. I just happened to walk in quietly on this conversation. Sharon was such a free spirit. I could see in her eyes that she may consider it.

I went into the room and said that is not going to happen at all. That baby has my blood running through his veins, and if he needs a home, he can stay with your father and me as our son. I told her that she would be your sister. I told Ellis that since he wanted to sell you that I'm sure he would not want to be around.

I turned around thinking the nurse was behind me, but it was dad. He said, 'I knew some kind of nonsense was happening around this baby boy. Sharon, you are free to do whatever you need to do for your life. I turned you over to God a long time ago. I have done all that I can to love you and provide a home, food, and clothing, but you continue to want to do things your way. You can come home and be a mother to this baby, or you can leave and go stay with one of your sisters or brothers, but you will not corrupt the soul and spirit of my grandson. God has a light over his life, and I saw it when I laid eyes on him for the first time. I just spoke with the doctor, and he said you are able to leave today. All of us are going to leave and give you and dummy a chance to think about what I have said, but my grandbaby is not for sale and if I have to take you all to court to keep him I will. Got me?' I stood beside dad, and I was so proud of him making this declaration of love for our grandson."

"Eli do you have any questions for us?"

"No, ma'am."

"Are you mad at us?"

"How could I be angry at two people that have shown me so much love and gave me a solid foundation for my life?"

"Honey, we just wanted to make sure nothing came out that you were unaware of. I don't want anything to startle you on your special day."

I hugged them both and asked if I could go to my room.

When I got to my room, I saw how blessed I was. There was nothing that I did not have in my room and its always been that way. I thought about how much I looked like Sharon, and I often wondered why we favored so much. When I am with her, she always looks at me with those big loving eyes. She always sent me cards and little things, and she actually was at a lot of games when I was in middle school. Honestly, she was doing what sisters do for the youngest sibling. I asked myself if I was mad and I wasn't. I wondered why a man that has a baby would want to sell it instead of raising it. I am not that man. No matter what, I thought of my wonderful upbringing, and that alone crushed the negativity of the news.

I was so hungry. I went down stairs and ran right into Sharon.

"There is my big man!" Something that she has always said my entire life.

We chatted for a little bit. She said she wanted to share something with me, but my dad chimed in, "Let's eat everyone."

Its been a long time since we have all sat around this table at the same time. Dang momma, threw down today. Fat and happy is what we all were.

I went to school the next morning for graduation rehearsal, and then they let the seniors go home. I decided to go to Mr. Garrett's class to really look at him. He was so happy to see me.

He said, "Boy I thought I wouldn't see you again until tomorrow at graduation."

"I just wanted to swing by and say hey. Thanks for always being a part of my life and such a great teacher. It really did not dawn on me until yesterday that you have taught at every school that I have gone to from elementary all the way to high school. I have always been in your class at some time of the year."

Mr. Garrett, just looked at me as if he knew that I had learned of our connection. He cleared his throat and said, "It has been a blessing to watch my students grow up into fine young men and women, but you Eli remind me of my son. I admire the path that you have taken in life. I wish my son had adhered to the life that his mother and I had provided for him. You respected your parents out of their presence, and that young man shows a sign of character and honor. I appreciate you for that behavior."

I got back home, and Sharon and a man were on the front porch listening to music. The man looked like my twin, so I wondered if that was my biological father. They both looked at me with big crazy eyes. The man just blurted out, "I am your real father and the man you call dad is your grandfather."

Sharon looked at him and said, "I thought we were going to wait until after graduation. You are so inconsiderate."

"So who is my mother sir if you are my father?"

Sharon said, "I am Eli. She went through the long story that my parents already told me."

I said smugly, "I already know. My parents cared enough about my special day not to allow me to have this possible disruption. Know this both of you; I appreciate you giving me life and handing me over to my mom and dad. I don't have any ill will towards either of you. Just know that whatever I have accomplished in life is due to the upbringing of my mom and dad and the rest of my brothers and sisters.

So, if you are expecting to do anything legally towards us, think twice. I will be eighteen in four days, and you have no rights to me, my life or my money.

Sharon as my sister you have been a jewel and I would like to keep it that way. Dude, I don't know you from a hole in the wall, but I do accept Mr. Garrett as I know he is your father. He has been a wonderful, supportive person in my life. What man would switch schools every three years just to be near their grandson? A good and honorable man. I plan on keeping him in my life since his wife has passed.

Peace out Sharon. I am going to see some of my friends to fix the tops of our graduation hats. Mom wanted to do it, but man, she wanted to put a baby sock on there and some other crap. Ummm No!"

Family secrets don't always end up in a good place like this one. When I have kids, who's to say that I won't sweep that family secret under the rug for the safety of my children?

THE SECRET OF SEXUAL ADDICTION

The Need to be One with Another Person on the Deepest Level with No Regard for Your Damaged Soul

"Mom, today is the fair on the lake can we go!"

"Ralph you know we have your ball game this morning."

"I mean, can you take us after the match and Sissy's tutoring class?"

"It is a beautiful day so why not? Yes, love we can go!" The fair would be a welcomed break from my thoughts today.

As we pulled into the ball field one of the parents immediately started screaming my name, she saved me a shaded seat on the bench.

"Charity, why are you guys late?"

"Elaine, we are about four and half minutes late, shut up."

She laughed because she says I get up before the roosters, and I am an over achiever just because I am always early to every event.

"Crazy Girl!"

Corrine, my baby girl, came over to get money for the concession stand.

"Really, Corrine we just got here."

"I want a juice, momma." Who could deny that sweet little face? Ralph was almost ten, and Corrine was five.

Elaine wanted to talk about her escapades with her numerous nighttime boy toys. She was so open about it all. Thank goodness practice was over, and the tutor sent a text stating that she would not be able to tutor Corrine today. Yes!

I bet you are wondering why Corrine needs a tutor at five. It is not academic; she is as smart as a whip. This kid wants to be a track and field hurdle jumper when she grows up but is convinced that she needs to be able to do a split perfectly. She doesn't feel that the gymnastics coach is doing enough to help her reach her goals. Yes, she is five, but who am I to knock a kid's dreams.

We were driving with the windows down, the sky was beautiful, and the temperature was perfect. I always listened to jazz, so the kids never argued with that. Ralph knew that the music soothed the sadness in my eyes, his words.

"So momma, are you all right?" He asked.

"Yes, love I am perfect. How are you?"

"I'm good, mom, but I will be better when I am able to get a big fat cotton candy and a hot dog from the fair."

I was looking forward to it more than they could imagine. I wanted a candy apple and a snow cone.

Corrine was singing, "Brother is going to win me a new toy. Throw that ball, throw that ball, knock it down and get my prize. Hahaha!" She cracks me up.

We got there, and it was already a good crowd. We ran into my friend Ivan, and he walked with us and helped Ralph win Corrine a few new stuffed animals. It was nice. I really wanted to ride the Ferris Wheel. I wanted to be there alone for just a moment to gather my thoughts. Ivan took the kids to the hot dog stand and let me ride. As the Ferris Wheel began to move the breeze caressed my face and my thoughts. I breathed so deeply that it made me light headed.

Please tell me why this machine stopped working after I reached the very top. I wanted to panic, but I looked down at the people and spotted Ralph. Ralph was so unique to me; he was the product of a vicious attack on my body and soul. I could have aborted him, but I could not do it. Through my suffering, God blessed me with a beautiful son that resembled the sun every time he looked at me and smiled. There were no feelings of anger or sadness when I looked at him, just love. It could have been the other way, but thankfully, it wasn't. Corrine was the product of a one-night stand because of my inability to know love without sleeping with it. My life and men, God, help me.

As I sat there and looked at Ivan with my kids, I was amazed at the loving care that he showed them. Ivan was too good for me. My body constantly craved the wrong man and the wrong thing. He was God fearing, loving, no kids and a hard worker. What the hell is wrong with me? All I could think about was getting these kids to my mother's house for the rest of the weekend.

Finally, the winds begin to hit me in the face for the fast ride to the bottom. My kids and Ivan were standing on the bottom looking up at me. Ralph looked like, how cool is that that I was suspended in the air; Corrine looked like she had to tinkle, and Ivan's eyes looked like he was terrified but full of love. No one has ever looked at me the way he does. I wonder does he even know how he looks at me.

I can't think of him. I have a hot date with a guy I met through a friend. He has a reputation of being a lady's man, but I need to see for myself if the hype is true. I dropped the kids off with my mother and went in and sat with her for a second. Of course, she made reference to my bland outfit.

"Good grief Charity, did you wear that long-sleeved shirt to the ball field and the fair? Girl you totally need to come out of the black and the work clothes it's the freaking weekend. Charity for crying aloud put on some dang color. I do not know how you are my daughter sometimes."

My mom was full of color and fashionable clothes. Man, if I could see her just once without her referencing my style of dress, it would be a blessing to my ears. My kids were excited to be at moms because the community has a lot of kids and a community pool with a lifeguard. There's only me to protect them at home in our pool, and there are not a lot of kids. I have been thinking about moving, but for once in my life, I feel safe in this house and in this neighborhood, so moving is not in sight right now.

"See you tomorrow babies! They were already changing to go outside to see their friends."

My mom chimed in and said, "Who wants to stay the week with Grandma?"

Without hesitation, the choir sang, "We do!"

"Wow, no one wants to stay with me?" They came up and loved on me and said they just wanted to hang with Granny before we went on vacation.

Ralph whispered in my ear, "I can come home with you if you will be lonely."

"No baby, you stay and have fun, and I will finish up my eBook."

Ralph and I are writers, and he is magnificent. We decided to write an eBook and have it published. He finished his and I have been a slacker. That is funny. This guy won't even put his clothes away, but he can finish a forty page story on how to train for a baseball tournament. On top of that, he found a person that will format it for us to put it online. My dude!

Corrine finally came up, and I thought she was going to love on me, but she said, "Mom, please bring my doll and her clothes over here, and I need a few more outfits by Tuesday. Oh, you will be okay without me so just work on your book and get it finished before I get home." Two entirely different kids but I need them both in my life.

What a welcomed surprise for me. I took off work for the summer so that I could be with the kids so this is a great break. I got home and fixed me a huge glass of tea, put on some saxophone jazz, sat on my deck, and looked at the fish in the coy pond. I was on my phone, and when I looked up, the twinkle lights were on. Goodness! I have been sitting here for at least two hours. A deer was staring at me like feed me, woman. Crap, my deer feeders were empty. Sorry baby doe, I will feed you tomorrow.

My work phone started to ring, so I jumped up to grab it. Why is it ringing and I am off?

"This is Charity."

A deep sexy voice came over the line and said, "Hello Charity, I just wanted to make sure we were still on for dinner and drinks tonight."

"Oh, hello Thomas how are you. This is my work line I almost did not answer the phone."

"This was the only number your home girl gave to me."

"That's cool. Where would you like to meet?" I asked.

"So you don't want me to come and pick you up?"

" I would prefer to meet you if that is okay."

"Okay, mystery lady. Let's meet at Jazzy's Dinner Club on forty-seventh and Brunswick. Have you ever been there?"

"I have not, but it was on my list to do this summer. What time would you like to meet?"

"How about 8pm?"

"I will see you there Thomas."

I took a long hot shower and put on a beautiful black lace bra and panty set with a sexy pair of thigh high silk to the touch stockings. I went into my private closet which had another private room off from the closet. I turned my light on and chose a deep red form fitting dress, added some delicate jewelry and dark red lipstick. My hair was pulled up into a beautiful updo with large curls framing my face. My perfume was soft but seductive.

I got to the restaurant a little earlier than Thomas so that I could decide my after dinner move when he walked in. The bar faced the door, so I sat down and talked with the bartender. I had only seen a picture of Thomas so when I looked up and saw this tall, beautiful, dark, man with a smile that could stop traffic swagger his way towards me, my body said yes indeed, it is on tonight. Thomas greeted me with a hug and a kiss on the cheek. Damn, he smelled good.

The hostess came with him to seat us near the stage so that we could enjoy the jazz band.

When I stood up, he said, "Dang Charity you are sexy as hell." He looked at me with that look I knew all too well. Mr. Fine thought he was going to have some of me tonight, and he was so right.

As soon as we were seated, the server came to take our drink orders. Both of us were hungry, so we got an appetizer and checked out their dynamic menu. He ordered for me, which was cool. The band began to play as soon as our food came. We had an excellent conversation and a lot of laughter. Maybe I should not put him in my web of shame. He smelled so good, though. I'm in a dilemma here. Last week the guy was great and so sweet. I just couldn't imagine being with him on a regular basis, but we had a good time, we went straight to a hotel, and I went home. He has called a hundred times this week. Whatever, I am not interested.

The guy I was with the week before that, I can't even remember his name. His sex game was on point but oh well. He was probably really nice, but I really do not remember anything except he was great in the sack. Thomas seems a little different from my many other conquests. I should leave him alone, have dinner, and go home.

Anyway, the band was fantastic. The saxophone player and the trumpet player were a great team. After dinner, Thomas asked me if I would like to go for a walk or for a ride. My mind immediately wandered if he wanted to take me for a ride in the car or a ride in the bed. I am so sick! I said, "let's walk." He paid the bill, and we took off down the street.

There were so many things still open on this little strip. It was pleasant, and the temperature was great. I was really happy when he saw an empty bench in front of a fountain that had various colors or water. We sat there, and he grabbed my foot, took off my shoe, and rubbed my feet, right there in the middle of this park.

"With shoes like those your feet had to have started hurting by now."

That was funny and so true. He was sweet and thoughtful.

"Charity, my condominium is across the street would you like to come in for a little while."

Okay there it is, I thought.

I said, "Sure that would be cool." I had not even noticed that this building was a housing unit. I thought it was a stacked mall. I'm so goofy!

We went across the street to his condo; on the first-floor were retail stores and an excellent bar.

He asked, "Would you like to have a drink here?"

"Sure."

The atmosphere was fantastic. The server was very informative about their new mixed drinks created by their mixologist. I opted to stay true to my real boyfriend, Jack.

"Wow that is a strong drink for such a cute little lady."

He joined Jack and me and nearly gagged all the way through the drink. I thought that was funny. He was a straight wine drinker. They had some really nice music playing.

"Do you realize that you close your eyes when a saxophone comes on?" he asked thoughtfully.

"Really, I did not notice."

"You also sway from side to side." Okay, so he is very observant.

I am feeling so empty on the inside even though I look beautiful. I'm in a beautiful place, with a handsome man that smelled like a saxophone made me feel on the inside. Warm, seductive, and inviting. My mind wanted just to end the night and not go into his space, but my body was racing to see what he felt like even if we just danced.

"Are you ready to go up?" he asked.

"Okay."

I tried to help myself and him by telling him that I couldn't stay long.

"That's cool; when you are ready, we will walk back to your car."

He opened the door, and I walked into a beautifully decorated bachelor pad. He and his son LB were on every photo in the home. It was sweet. He showed me around and offered me more wine. I accepted, and we sat down on the couch and listened to some more music.

This was nice. My little voice said, *Charity, do not fall for this guy. Get what you want and bounce.*

As we sat there, we talked about his work.

"Please tell me how you were able to take a month off from the job?" he inquired.

"I am the world's biggest saver, and my company buys fine art and pottery for a couple of museums and retail stores."

"Did you tell me you work for yourself or for a company?" I asked.

"I work for myself, actually. I started my business when I was about thirty so for the past seven years I have been on my own. Corporate decided to release me from my position of fifteen years, so I had to figure it out, without taking time away from my kids."

Thomas asked if I would like to dance. This was different.

"Sure."

Before I stood up, he said, "Wait right there."

He reached down and removed my shoes and then held his hand out. A beautiful piece came on, and he held me so gently as we rocked back and forth in a melodic rhythm that set my soul on fire. He could feel it too because his next question was, "Would you like to see my bedroom?"

"Yes, I would."

Usually, you would walk into the room, but this guy picked me up and carried me into the bedroom as if I were his bride being taken across the marriage threshold. He laid me down on his huge beautiful custom-made bed. The headboard was crafted with the most beautiful oriental designs. The bed looked as if it was wall to wall. I thought of all of the things that we could do in this bed to leave him happy and satisfied. Unlike, my many conquests this is new for me.

Thomas asked, "Do you mind if I change clothes?"

"No, not at all," I replied.

He disappeared into the closet, and honestly, I thought he was going to come back naked, but he came out in a tank and a pair of sweats.

"Would you like some sweats to put on or are you comfortable."

"No, I'm good" because I knew I looked freaking hot under this dress.

He lay down beside me, propped his head up on his hand, and just looked at me. I asked him about his son LB. We talked about him, his mother, and his school. Thomas and I talked for about three hours before I noticed it was midnight, and I was still dressed. Wow! He did not try anything with me. I was not used to that.

I decided to see if he was a good guy or if he was putting on for me. I kissed him on the cheek, and he smiled and kissed me back on the check. Then I kissed him on the neck, and he reciprocated. My next move was on the lips, and he said, "Are you sure?"

"Yes, I am." When he kissed me it was so sweet and loving, I thought I would lose it if we did not move forward.

Get this; his next question was, "Are you ready to leave."

"No, not really do you want me too?"

He said "No. Would you like to stay with me tonight?"

There it is I thought.

"Sure that would be okay."

He gave me a pair of sweats and a T-shirt and said here you go. I got up and began to change. He watched me standing there in my lace bra and panties with my silky thigh high stockings. I left my bra and panties on and slid on the sweat pants and shirt.

He said, "Now you know you want to take that doggone bra off. I know how you all do. That is the first thing you sling off when you get home." We both burst into laughter.

I was thankful because I really did not expect to still be in that bra at this time tonight. I could not figure this out; I was in uncharted territory. Most men jump on my bus as soon as we hit the bed.

Thomas said, "Let me show you something."

We went to the hallway which led up to the rooftop of the building. There was a rooftop pool and an artificial grass area. It was beautiful. The sides of the building had so many tiny lights that accented the beautiful glow of the moon. We sat down at the pool and put our feet in. We laughed and talked so much I felt like I was home.

"Charity, I left our drinks in the house would you like something?"

"I am quite thirsty and a little hungry."

He left and came back with some snacks and wine. I looked all in the bottom of my glass for any unusual bubbles or anything. I have been drugged once by my conquest who had no idea that he was going to get laid without the drug. I still ended up leaving his behind the same night after it was over and he was the one sleep.

"I did not put anything in your drink Charity." I couldn't help but laugh.

The next thing we knew it was 3am. He said, "I'm tired what about you?"

"I am so tired."

We went back to the house and got in bed. He looked at me with those beautiful dark eyes and said, "I sleep without a shirt is that cool."

"Hey, it's your crib do what you want brother."

He pulled me to him and caressed my hair so gently. I went to sleep, and through the night I could hear him say, "This feels so good."

I was sweltering at one point in the night, so I took off the T-shirt. Oh my goodness, to feel his skin on mine made me think I was in love. I slept like a brick the rest of the night.

I woke up to the beautiful aroma of a deeply blended coffee. Yes, I do know my coffees. I went to the restroom, and he had laid out everything I needed to get cleaned up. He also put out another set of clothes for me to put on. That was sweet.

"Charity.", He called from the kitchen. "Are you hungry?"

"Yes, I am!"

He had already cut up fresh fruit and toast.

"Are you little hungry or big hungry?"

"I am big hungry, Thomas."

He began to whip up omelets and added fresh vegetables, fresh toast and refilled my coffee. I could totally get used to this. Those eyes just looked at me and smiled so genuinely. We ate and talked a little more.

He said, "Give me your keys. I am going to jog and go get your car. Do you have extra shoes in there?"

"Yes, I have some flip-flops."

"Good, I don't want you taking the walk of shame down the street in that hot dress and those red bottoms you had on last night."

What is happening here, I thought. He is pulling me into his world with his music, sweet kisses, and gentle behaviors. While he was gone, I made the bed and cleaned the kitchen. It felt so good to feel like I was in a relationship even for one night.

I heard Thomas come in. He said, "Wow! You cleaned, impressive.

"It is the least I could do for your perfect behavior last night. I really had a great time with you, Thomas."

"We can have as many as you like."

"It is early Saturday morning, so maybe I should leave you to carry on with your day."

"Well if you don't have any plans, maybe we can take a walk or go to that little coffee shop I saw you eyeing last night near Jazzy's."

"You saw that?"

"Umm, you almost made me step in a pool of your saliva when you saw that double chocolate muffin. Not to mention how your eyes closed when you smelled the coffee."

I am amazed at this man at this moment. It happened, I felt it in my soul, my guard was down, and my heart was opened. The thoughts of being left and reaping the seeds I've sown with the men I have hurt flew into my mind.

"Thomas, I really need to get home but may I call you later?"

"Sure, how about dinner tonight on the roof, we will grill."

Oh my goodness, what is happening here?

It was like I was having an out of body experience because the next thing I heard was, "That sounds great what time? Would you like for me to bring something?"

"How does 6pm work for you? Just bring that smile, those eyes, and your appetite."

He walked me to my car and kissed me so sweetly on my forehead. I'm scared.

On the way home I decided to go to that coffee shop and get that muffin and some of that delightful aroma of coffee. While I was sitting there, I went back over the evening and wondered how I let this happen. He came into my heart and not my body. He treated me better than I treat myself. Surely something is wrong with him or am I moving too fast?

Over the past few years, I have lived a double life. I portrayed a plain, hardworking, successful business woman, and hands-on momma. I had a standing babysitter two nights a week, and I would take that time to go out and feel the touch and kiss of a stranger. Someone that may have been as wounded as me and just needed to be connected for one night. I let these men know up front that I did not want a relationship and if they were down for a hookup, that was cool. If they wanted a wife or girlfriend, to please keep it moving. I am not that girl. I did not feel worthy of a relationship. My body was destroyed as a child and teenager against my will, so how in the world do I quit allowing myself to be used and abused.

In the past, someone else decided to hurt me, and now I am hurting myself to fill the void of a loss of self-love, self-respect and the belief that someone could love me without wanting my body. I have hurt some with my ability to sleep with them today and say, please do not call me again as soon as I get in my car. One man told me that I would get mine one day, and he hopes I hurt as bad as I hurt him. I called him on his so-called pain. I told this dude that just because he was the big man in his area and all of the women fell to his feet and stalked him, I wasn't. Yeah, big boy, I checked you out. So don't be mad at me for giving you a taste of your own medicine. By the way, your sex game is on point. Bye! His mouth was left on the floor.

As I drove home, I thought, what if Thomas is going to pay me back in some way. I am fearful of everything, but I have the courage to deal with whatever life brings me. I am going to ride it out and see what happens with him. One thing happened to me last night that was awesome; I was able to just be, even though I was waiting for something to happen, it did not. It was nice, and I felt for a moment that I could trust the situation and possibly him.

My home was my safety zone, yet I had a secret closet that held risqué clothes that were beautiful in color and style. One day I saw one of my mother's friends while I was on a date and I was in a white dress with red jewelry, red shoes, and my hair was curled beautifully. I saw her, but I looked so different that she did not think she knew me, so I did not speak to her. My mom called me that night and asked me what did I did that evening. I told her I was at the bookstore until they closed. She told me what her friend said about the woman she saw that was so beautiful. My mother told her, "Oh I know that wasn't Charity because everything in her house is beige, brown or cream all the way down to her clothes." This woman! I had to laugh at myself. Why have I hidden my great fashion sense and saved it only for dates with men that I have no intention of being with long term?

I sat down in the kitchen and looked out at the pool and daydreamed for about an hour about much of nothing. I went to the gym and worked out and sat in the steam room for a bit. Totally relaxed. It was only 1pm so I watched some Lifetime. There was a story on there about the secret pain a prostitute feels or something. I fell in line with the life of a prostitute without getting paid. Wow! At least most prostitutes are out there because they need an income or they are being forced and do not have anyone in their lives to help them get out of that life. What am I doing? I should be ashamed of myself and get some help. I certainly can't go to my pastor or mother for help. I am not in the mood to be judged. I just want this roller coaster of men and illicit sex to stop. It is not serving anyone or helping me understand how to control it.

I was getting hungry, but I wanted to make sure I would be able to eat something at dinner. I was totally looking forward to seeing him tonight. My cell rang, and it was Ralph.

"Hey, momma are you okay?"

"Yes, baby I am good."

He said, "Turn on your video and let me see you." Good grief this dude acts like my daddy for sure, but I love it. I turned it on, and the first thing he said was whose shirt is that.

"Where?"

He said, "Across the back of the couch."

"Dang, dude, it's my shirt."

"Oh okay, I have never seen that shirt mom."

"Ralph where is Corrine."

"That girl is over Megan and Victoria's house."

"How has she been acting?"

"Sharp-tongued and crazy but Granny has got the same type of tongue she has so they go back and forth all the time. It's funny to me, so I just keep playing my game and tune them completely out."

"Momma, I saw Mr. Ivan at the store, and he told me to tell you hello. He said he would take me to practice on Saturday so Grandma or you would not have to do it."

"That's sweet of him. Are you cool with that?"

"Yes, momma, I like him, he is cool."

"What are you going to do for dinner tonight?"

Before I knew it, I told him that a friend of mine was going to grill out, and I would be eating at his house?

"Back up lady, you have a date?"

What is happening to me, I just told my ten year old I have a date. As far as he knows, he is the only man in my life.

He said, "Thank goodness I was starting to think you were going to be an old maid."

"What boy!"

"That's what Grandma says every time we spend the night."

He told me to have fun and video chat him so he can take up for me when Grandma talks about my clothes and the fact that I don't do anything.

"Will do Sir Ralph." I love this little guy.

My Corrine is so strong willed I admire her ability at five to be her own person and make pretty good decisions about what she wants to do. She sticks to it no matter what her little entourage is doing. She is stronger than I was at five and Ralph is the first male that really cares about me. After speaking with Ralph, courage of change came over me. I put on some Kirk Whalum and poured a big glass of sweet tea and went into my secret closet. I looked at some of the clothes and thought, good grief you look like a hooker in this compared to the woman that you are on a daily basis.

These colors are the true me, and I am not this bland and boring person. I think I went this route to cover up the fact that I am a passionate, vibrant woman that wants to experience life to the fullest. Why would I hide this side of me from the world? No one knows my story but me, so why hide who am? Am I trying to fool the world or myself? This is stupid! I took those clothes out and kept the clothes that looked sexy but sophisticated. I boxed those up, but I'm too embarrassed to give them away. I did keep the lingerie because I love beautiful undergarments no matter what I was wearing on the outside.

After boxing up what I wanted to get rid of, I started thinking about what I would wear tonight. I found a yellow sundress that was so comfy and yet elegant. I even had a pair of yellow heels to go with it. My mom wears flowers in her hair, and I thought, maybe I should put something in my hair. One of my clients gave me this diamond looking headband, and it had hints of yellow in some of the stones. I looked like Pocahontas. This was fun, looking forward to a date who so far wanted nothing from me but to please me.

God, please help me change my life. I don't want to live the life I have been living anymore. I don't want to be hurt by this man and abandoned by love or the thoughts of love. For once in my life, I am completely excited about Thomas. It's like I have known him in a life that allowed me to know love. My phone was ringing, and it startled me. Good grief, I was deep in thought. It was Thomas.

"Hey,pretty lady! I just wanted to make sure you were not going to stand me up or anything."

"No, I wouldn't do that. I am hungry, and I'm getting dressed."

"Oh, do you like hummus?"

"Yes, I do."

"Awesome I made some fresh."

"Well alright Chef Thomas, see you at six."

"You can come now if you like."

"I am coming on then. See you in a bit."

It was so nice outside, and I felt so good. Oh crap, I forgot to video chat with Ralph. Wait until he sees this color on his momma.

As soon as the first ring went through, he answered and said, "I thought you forgot. Wait, who are you, lady? Mom is that you?"

"Yes, baby, it's me."

"Mommy, you look so beautiful! Send me a photo so I can put it on my phone and tablet."

"Ok, I will, "I said with a smile.

"Momma have fun tonight with this mystery date. Love you."

"Ralph wait, where is Corrine?"

"She and Grandma are at some girl's toe and nail party next door."

"You are alone? Are you okay?"

"Mom, I am almost eleven. I am playing my game and eating all of these treats Granny made. I'm good!"

"Okay, I will call you tomorrow. Please let Corrine know I asked about her and tell her little butt to call me."

I got in the car and headed towards the cute little eclectic street that Thomas lived on. I thought I would stop at the coffee shop and pick up a pound of their delicious blend and a couple of those double chocolate muffins. I like what I like though. When I got there, the stores were still open, and I wanted to pick up something to take. There was a florist shop that had some beautiful flowers that would look beautiful in his foyer. So I picked them up and hoped he liked them.

Just as I was about to get onto the elevator, it opened, and he was in it.

"Hey, Thomas!"

He grabbed me and hugged me like he missed me or something. I wanted to cry. When you are not used to real love or real affection, it feels weird, but it also feels so good.

We got on the elevator, and he said, "May I kiss you Charity?"

I just nodded, and he gently held my face in both hands and kissed me so gently and passionately I felt like my knees would buckle under me. I could barely open my eyes as I heard the elevator open. He must have felt the faintness of my body, so he held my hand as we got off the elevator.

He asked, "So are those flowers for me?"

"Yes, I thought they would be pretty on this table."

We went into the kitchen which smelled fantastic. My stomach was growling like a bear, and he heard it.

"Oh my, was that your stomach Charity?"

I was so embarrassed.

"Yes."

He moved a platter of red pepper hummus and some pita chips in front of me and poured me a glass of Riesling. I sat on the stool at the island and munched away. He got a vase from the cabinet and put the flowers in it and sat them on the table in the foyer.

"Thanks, honey these look great in here. Are you ready to eat?"

"Yes, I am!"

We went into the bedroom.

"We are eating in here?"

"Yes, we are going to watch an Empire Marathon."

"Wow!"

Thomas was quite the cook. We had steaks with grilled corn, zucchini and squash and a sweet potato. I didn't tell him that this is my favorite meal. We ate, drank and watched my favorite show. My fear is heightened because we click so well. Why am I waiting for the bottom to fall out of this two-day harmonious relationship? The question came quickly; "Can you stay with me tonight Charity?"

"Yes, Thomas I even packed an overnight bag." He was so excited. It has only been two days, but it feels like a lifetime. I stuffed my face so much, and I was so full.

"Great meal Chef!"

"Wait until you see what I made for dessert."

We took our plates to the kitchen and refilled our glasses and got back on the bed to watch more of my show. We were so fat and happy that we both fell asleep. When we woke up, it was almost 10pm. Dang, it's late.

Thomas asked, "Do you want to go for a swim?"

That sounded like a plan to me. I did not bring my bathing suit, but he handed me a bag, and in it was a fly bikini.

He said, "I hope it's not too big."

Is he trying to make me love him? I went into the bathroom and put it on. It was a perfect fit. I thought this man has skills. He grabbed a couple of bottles of water, and we caught the elevator up to the roof. The weather had calmed down, and the breeze from being so high up was great. We stayed in the pool and laughed and talked. Soon it was midnight.

He said, "Come on momma let's go in and have some dessert."

We showered and changed clothes, and I put on my yoga gear. When I came out of the bathroom, he brought a huge strawberry cheesecake to share. This evening could not have been any more perfect.

You would think that we would be wide awake after sleeping for almost three hours, not so much.

"Thomas, asked again if he could kiss me."

I thought, please do it. He kissed me and held me. I could not contain myself. I wanted to make love to him so badly, but he did not have it. He told me that he did not want us to be that couple that gets along so good, and sex ruins it. Okay, I'm done! I am laughing at myself because this is the first time in years that I have been with a man and nothing sexual has happened. This is new territory for me. I want him to finish this because this has turned emotional, and I am falling for him, which is not my style. Why can't I just let someone love me and why can't I trust that it is real love.

As I looked into his eyes and felt his hands on my back, I thought I would explode. I knew if he did not make a move I would so I said, "Let's go clean the kitchen. I will cook for you in the morning."

I'd brought in the muffins and the coffee in my huge bag. He got on his knees and said, "Get on my back." He piggybacked me into the kitchen, living room, foyer and guest room and back to the kitchen. This dude is crazy. We cleaned the kitchen, and I laid the muffins and coffee out of my bag.

Thomas grabbed a remote, and Brian Culbertson came on a nice and slow melodic tune. We danced, and he picked me up and sat me on the counter and begin kissing me all over. I wanted to remind him of what he said about sex ruining what we have, but I could not say a word. He pulled my shirt off, and he carried me to the living room. We lay on the carpet, and he took off all of my clothes and loved me. He didn't have sex with me, rape me, molested me, but he loved me. Not sure if I had ever felt this way in my entire life. When all was said and done, we took a shower together and went to bed. I was complete in my heart and satisfied in my body.

Thomas is a keeper. We dated for a year almost, and it was great. My son liked him a little, but Corrine, of course, was like NO in all caps! Then it happened. We were supposed to go out and celebrate his birthday, but he was a no-show. He texted me some vague text about his back hurting. Then the next two days I did not hear from him. That is when he texted me to tell me that he had reconnected with a woman he was in love with from high school. Wow, this totally cannot be happening. I went against my better judgment to allow him inside of my world, my heart, and my trust. Just like that, it was over.

I went to his house to collect my things. He held me and said it had nothing to do with our relationship, but he just needed to see if there was something there with this girl. As tough as I could be, I said that's cool. I left about an hour or so later, and that was that.

My secret life was no longer needed after I learned that pain is pain whether you allow someone to inflict it upon you, or you inflict it upon yourself. All these years I thought I was sleeping around because I needed to feel as one with someone even if it were for one night or few hours. After a long life of being messed with from a child all the way through my adult life, I am tired of giving myself away without the possibility of having that one someone in my life. Then I met Thomas, and he showed me what it felt like to have someone pursue me and love me with the simple things in life: good conversation, laughter, good food, great music and good loving.

The fact of the matter is, I have never felt I was good enough for anyone to love. There was always something that was wrong with me to where I had to give myself to get anything in return. Then I wondered, was it a sexual addiction that I had or was it the lack of love that was missing? It is so easy to confuse sex for love. When I was giving myself away, I convinced myself that it was sex because I just wanted it but really, it was sex with the internal feeling of being loved. I am empty in the love department except for the love my kids have for me. My workload and kids' activities have picked up so much that I do not have time to think about love, sex or anything.

I thought I would do something with some of the buyers from some other companies. These ladies were experts in their business and knew the ends and outs of it all. Cassandra, Gail, Shayla, Regina, and April, I called them the Fabulous Five. We went out for dinner and drinks. All of them were married and happy, so I learned a lot by listening to them talk about the ins and outs of marriage. How every day would not be a bed of roses, but the multitude of thorns is what makes it grow stronger and last. I have never been married, so this was an impressive knowledge for me to pick up on. Just in case God sends someone my way.

When I got home, Ivan called me and asked me if he could spend some time with my son this following weekend. I said sure and asked if there was anything wrong. I thought I had missed something.

He said, "You didn't miss anything. His birthday is coming up, and he will be twelve, so it's time to have some conversations or at least be available if he wants to talk about anything without you or Corrine being around."

I really appreciate Ivan. He is always there for me when I need him to help me with the kids or if I need help around the house. I wonder why he isn't married. I don't think he and I have ever really been alone to chat, and I have known him for about four years. He is a teacher during the day, and he has an online investment thing he does in the evening. He is very wealthy and handsome. One thing I have noticed lately is the look Corrine gets on her face when Ivan is coming towards her when we see him. Heck, she doesn't look like that when I'm coming. Did I just get jealous? I think I did. Maybe I should get him a gift to show my gratitude for his help with these kids all of these years.

I do know that he is a lover of waterfalls and hiking trails. While I was out buying for one of my clients, I saw this photo that had an amazing waterfall on it that flowed into a bright blue wading lake; the waterfall is surrounded by beautiful greenery and dirt trails. I think he would like this gift from the kids.

That night when I got home, I asked Ralph and Corrine if they would like to fix dinner for Ivan and give him a gift for being such a good father figure for them.

Corrine said that would be great mom and Ralph asked if we could grill for him and have it by the pool? I showed them the picture, and they loved it. I called him and asked if he would be available for a cookout on Saturday by the pool.

"That sounds great. Would you like for me to bring anything?"

"Nothing at all. The kids have already made a shopping list, and they have so much on it. Can just come around noonish? If you want to bring a date you can, I will just let the kids know to make room for one more."

"No Charity, I do not have anyone special in my life that I would want to remotely introduce to the kids." Dang, he said that like my kids were his kids. That was so sweet and sincere.

My mom has been off of my back since I came out of my private life of color and sexcapades. Yes, I made that word up. She is actually treating me differently and so much better. My lack of color in my personality and clothes made her treat me harshly, and my lack of love made me treat myself harshly. Well, that life is over for both of us. I still have no love for another person but I at least love myself now, and that has made everything change. Life was on the upswing.

Early Saturday morning Ralph and Corrine were up and planning the day for Ivan. I made the potato salad and slaw, and Corrine ordered a double chocolate cake from the bakery at the grocery store. Ralph was grilling the hot dogs. He said that Ivan liked the Polish sausages, so he put some of those on the grill. Corrine asked me if they could put the corn and some veggies on a stick. "Ivan does not eat bread, so we don't need that much out here except for us, she said."

I was a servant, and they were the executives for this cookout from the menu to the set up to the drinks. Ralph even wrote down a beer that he saw Ivan drink from a photo he had shown them of his family gathering. Wow. They loved him!

Everything was ready to go, and the doorbell rang. Ralph let Ivan in and brought him into the kitchen where I was. He had the biggest bouquet of flowers, my favorite to be exact. Then he had a small bouquet for Corrine and a new mitt for Ralph. Out of all the years, we have known each other; I think this is the first time he has been in our home.

"Charity, you have a beautiful home."

Corrine said, Would you like to look around. I drew you a picture in my room."

I went with them but let her be the tour guide. She showed every room but mine. She said, "Mom can you show him your room, I need to go and check on Ralphs cooking."

She is so funny and mature. So, I took him into my room, and his eyes bucked a little.

"What's wrong?"

He said, "I have this exact bed in my bedroom."

My bed was a king sized bed with an oak canopy, huge dressers, and the television came up from a case at the foot of the bed. Everything in my room was cream colored and overstuffed for comfort. He saw my fireplace and said I was thinking about moving just so I could have a fireplace in my bedroom. I took him into the bathroom. My bathroom is one of my favorite places as it holds a sauna and a two-person shower with a waterfall in the center. The bathtub was a jet tub near the window that has a television in it with a small wine and water cooler. Off from that was my gym in which you could get into from the hallway also.

He said, "I could live in here."

"I really needed a place that was peaceful," I replied.

There was a double door off from the bedroom that leads to my private screened in porch which had the best sofa, and love seat, lamps and bird feeders were everywhere. I love animals. The breeze in that room was amazing even if it was hot. If it was too warm for me and my hot flashes, there were two ceiling fans to circulate some air. It was nice.

"Charity, why are you still single?"

"Wow, Ivan, I think it is because I actually just started to love myself and honor the fact that everything that has happened in my life was to make me stronger not destroy me."

"Where are the kid's father?"

Now I wasn't ready to discuss that with him and thank God Ralph came on the intercom to state that lunch was ready.

I said, "We had better get down there. They have put in a lot of work for you today."

Corrine brought the picture she drew down to the table because she forgot to show him during the tour. It was a picture of the four of us as a family. My heart was about to burst because I thought a man like him couldn't want a woman like me. That negative self-talk kicked into high gear when I saw the picture. I just smiled and said, "That is sweet honey."

Ivan, on the other hand, gave her the biggest hug and asked Corrine how he could let mommy know that he would love to make this photo a reality. She said, "Just tell her."

"Corrine do you even know what reality means."

"Sure, mom, it means to make it true."

"Excuse me, little smarty pants."

 I love her.

Ivan grabbed my hand and got on one knee and said, "Charity, I have loved you from the moment that I met you. I love these kids as my own, and I want to ask you to allow me the time to get to know more about you, and if you feel as close to me as I do you, we can make this picture a reality."

Ralph and Corrine are standing behind him with their hands in a praying position.

"Ivan I would love to give us an opportunity to get to know each other. We are already co-parenting, so I trust that part of you already," we laughed. I said, "If you got on one knee just to ask me for a relationship opportunity, what are you going to do when you ask me to marry you?"

He said, "Your mind can't conceive that just yet." I think I just felt the love in my heart.

I must say that Ralph and Corrine made this day beautiful. They went in the house while we were talking and brought out his gift. When he opened it, I believe I saw a tear fall from his eyes. He loved it so much.

He said, "You guys can come over and help me find a place to hang it, and I will cook for you all." They looked at me, and I said, that would be great.

The doorbell was ringing so I went to see who it was. It was my mom.

"Hey beautiful girl. I wanted to see if I could get the kids. There's a new movie out about a fish, and I want to see it and thought they might want to also."

I asked if she wanted anything to eat, Ralph had grilled some hotdogs, sausages, and hamburgers.

"That sounds good; I was waiting to eat to see if they would be hungry also."

"Grandma!!!"

"Hey babies, would you all like to go see the new fish movie and possibly spend the night so you can go to my church tomorrow? It is Children's Day."

"That sounds like fun mom can we go? Ivan can keep you company."

Mom greeted Ivan and said she was happy to see him over here. Interesting, did everyone see this jewel of a man and I didn't? I couldn't see the purity of Ivan because of the darkness that covered my soul. I glanced over at Ivan, and he was looking at me with so much love in his eyes, and I prayed right then and asked God not to let me be closed to him but be open to the gift of something real. When I looked back at him, I promise there was a ray of light over his head, and his eyes were screaming I love you to me. Mom ate and chatted while the kids gathered their things.

When they left, Ivan and I cleaned up the area and went inside. I asked if he would like to go and sit upstairs.

I said, "Oh, I forgot, would you like a beer?"

"How did you know I like beer?"

"Ralph saw a particular beer that you were drinking in a photo that you showed him, and he wanted you to have some here just in case you wanted one with lunch."

We stopped by the kitchen, and I got the beer from the fridge, and he was in awe. "You could barely see the label on that photo."

"Oh, try being a mom standing in the beer aisle at the grocery store with an eleven year old trying to find this beer. The looks and stares were crazy, but the look on your face made it worth it."

We went up to my room and sat on my balcony and turned the television. He said, "Let's listen to some music instead."

"Cool with me!"

He had a playlist of my favorite jazz artist. It was nice. We talked and laughed until it was dark outside. I heard my stomach growl, and so did he. He asked if I wanted to eat some more of the lunch or would I like to go out for a quick bite.

I said, "How about we order some Chinese food for delivery."

I was so comfortable and relaxed with him I didn't want to leave.

"Great, I will call the one that is a few streets away. They have the best egg rolls and orange chicken." He had that number on his phone.

I said, "Why do you have that number saved?"

He laughed and said, "I eat alone a lot, so I save my favorite places.

The food came, and we ate everything we ordered. I drank wine, and he drank his beer. He almost cried every time he took a sip.

"Why do you look at that bottle like that Ivan?"

He shook his head and said, "I have never really known love or had anyone that actually cared enough to make an entire day about me. I just feel completely happy in a place that joy has never reached from another human being. Charity, this is the beginning of the rest of our lives."

I felt that same way, and there were no hesitations or strings attached to the emotion. This felt so good to me.

He said, "Do you have any questions for me?"

I replied, "One. If we start on this journey together, and a woman from your past that you loved reappears, would you have to leave me to see what's up with her?"

"Charity, who does that to a woman that gives him her heart and trust? Life is not always greener on the other side. I would be foolish to leave a lady that I love and understand to be with a possibility of love and possibility of heartache."

I put my head on his shoulder, and he lifted my face and kissed me so passionately that I felt my forever in that kiss. Wait didn't I feel this with Thomas? I did, but this time, I feel it's real because I love myself now.

Ivan did not waste any time in moving our relationship forward. The next weekend the kids and I went to his parents' home, and they had a massive cookout. We met everyone in one swoop. The kids and his nieces and nephews acted as if they have known each other forever. His mom and sisters were so genuine and loved on my kids just as they did the rest. I felt like I was at home.

To my surprise, I looked up to see Thomas walking through the door. This is weird. Thomas was there with one of Ivan's cousins. They looked good together. I was happy for him. He looked at me like he had seen a ghost, though. I laughed to myself. Ivan came over and asked if I needed anything and to see if I was okay because he was playing cards with the men. He brought me a fresh glass of wine and kissed me right there in front of everyone.

His momma said, "Well alright Ms. Charity. You are the one! Ivan doesn't bring women to us and surely wouldn't kiss a lady in front of us. Welcome to the family baby girl."

When we got home the kids were beat so he carried Corrine in and put her on the bed, and I walked Ivan into his room. These folks were sleeping and sleep walking.

He came out and said, "I just took her shoes off and put her on the bed with her clothes. Thank you for going with me today. My family has texted me nonstop since we left talking about how wonderful you are. They are looking forward to seeing you and the kids again soon. Charity, I was thinking about us taking a vacation to the beach during the kid's spring break. What do you think?"

"That sounds great Ivan. Where will we go?"

"He said don't worry; I will take care of it. Just make sure you have all of your work caught up so you can enjoy it okay? One more thing Charity, I had something else planned, but I want to do this now."

We were standing in the living room, and it was quiet. My heart and soul were peaceful. He picked me up and sat me on his lap like a kid and said, "Do you have any idea of how much joy you bring me? Let me tell you. You have given my heart happiness that I have never felt with anyone in my entire life. Your very presence in the room makes me leap for joy within. When you smile at me, I want to grab you up and hold you. When you hug me, my entire body feels as if we are one. Those eyes make me melt every time. You bring me joy Charity, and I love you with my whole being. It takes so much more than love to make a relationship work, and I believe we have what it takes to build a stable home and foundation for our family. Do you feel any of this?"

As the tears streamed down my face, all I could do is lay back into his arms and cry. He held me so gently and rocked me until I could speak.

"Do you remember when you asked me about the kid's fathers?

"Yes."

"Well, Ralph is a product of a rape that I did not report, and Corrine is the result of a one-night stand. Throughout the entire time you have known me, I have suffered from what I thought was a sexual addiction issue, but it was a lack self-love. I have been with countless men, and I am ashamed. God has just recently brought me through the hard part of my life and showed me how to love me. I just want you to know this side of my past."

He said, "Charity. Do you feel this love I have for you now?"

"Yes," I said, softly.

"Do you know that I will love your kids as my own until I die?

"Yes."

"Do you know that I have enough love in my heart to help you work through anything you have going on within?

"Yes, okay, baby!"

"Charity, will you marry me?" He put a four-karat perfect ring on my finger.

"Ivan, yes I would love to be your wife."

He hugged me and kissed me so gently. "My love, I will see you tomorrow okay."

He did not even acknowledge my indiscretions or issues; he just acknowledged love.

Sunday morning I was up so early. I decided to fix the kids a big breakfast before church. I went to check on them, and Corrine had a fever and looked awful. I asked her if she was hungry and she said no. What! This kid never rejects food. Ralph, came in, and he looked tired too.

"Hmmm okay, I was going to fix us a big breakfast so we can go to church but from the looks of you two we need to stay home."

Ivan called, and I told him what was happening. He came right over with some soup, Tylenol, and juice. While I was nursing the kids he fixed me some coffee and bagels. Then he and the kids sat in the living room and watched Disney until Corrine fell asleep. I took a picture of this moment so I can remember it forever. Ralph laid on me, and he had a fever also. Yikes. I gave him some Tylenol and walked him to bed. Ivan and I sat on the couch and watched a repeat of Sunday Best, and to my surprise, he can sing. I told him I didn't want to stop him from going to church. He looked me in the eyes and said, "Our kids are sick. We will be missing church today. I can do a study if you like."

We studied about the Kingdom of God and how we were made in His image, but we don't walk in that authority. That was awesome. Then we sang a couple of songs and prayed right there in the living room on the couch. He is an excellent leader of a home and family. I am so full right now.

Then we heard a little voice that said, "Daddy, come up here."

He looked at me and tears were flowing. He practically ran upstairs and came back down with his baby girl. My daughter, our daughter. We loved on the kids all day and took turns going upstairs and cooking for each other. It was a perfect day. Ivan stayed the night, and we slept in my room on the balcony.

Corrine and Ralph woke us up fully dressed and asked if one of us take them to school. Dang, we were tired, but the kids were better. Amen!

The next week was spring break. That Sunday, Ivan texted me a list of clothing types to pack for the kids and me. He said to be ready by six on Monday morning. I will pick you up. I told the kids, and they were super stoked! "Mom this is like an adventure!"

I was excited because no one had ever done anything like this for me before, never ever. He was there on time, and we drove to the airport. He handed all of us our tickets, and as soon as we got through security, the flight was boarding. That almost never happens. The kids sat across from us on the plane with another child, so they enjoyed that a lot. Ivan and I chatted and enjoyed the flight also. Finally, we landed in Aruba. Oh my goodness, there was a car waiting for us at the airport that took us straight to our resort.

It was so cute because Ivan and Ralph had a room and Corrine and I had a room. They were connected to each other. We took a short rest, showered, and went to lunch. Ivan had a plan, and he knew his way around really good. I asked if he had been here before and he said no. He just studied the area of the resort and its surroundings.

After lunch, we walked to this beautiful shopping district and bought a few things. He bought the kids some really cute outfits and Corrine got a little tiara and some pearls. I thought that was strange, but she is a little princess. When we got back to the resort, everyone wanted to go to the pool and chill out. We changed and enjoyed the pool until dinner time. The kids were not ready to get out then. There was a restaurant close to the pool so we ate there so the children could get back in once their food is settled.

A couple hours later Ivan said, "Honey, I am going to take the kids for a little walk so you can relax for a minute alone." He called their names and gave them this look. They did not say a word but got their towels, put their flip flops on and waved bye to me. Okay, I am tired. I'm going to close my eyes for a second. In about an hour they returned, and Ivan said come on love let's call it a night. I have a lot planned for tomorrow. The boys went to their rooms and my baby, and I went to ours. She was out like a light, and so was I.

The next morning room service brought breakfast for all of us, and we ate well. Everything tasted so flavorful. Ivan disappeared for about forty-five minutes and when he returned he said, "Love I need you to do something for me. Everything I ask you to do, just do it for me, okay."

I said, "No problem you are the captain of this ship."

A woman came to the room and said, "Charity, come with me, please."

She took me to the spa. I had a full body massage, manicure, and pedicure. My hair was done in these whimsical curls, and a band of flowers was placed on my head. A server brought me a glass of wine and a note. It said, *Charity, today is the day I will make you my wife. Please continue to follow the direction of the ladies you are with right now, and they will bring you to me. I love you, and I will be waiting for you.*

I cried and was so happy. Traci and Angela were my ladies, and they were so sweet to me. My mom wasn't there to help me, but these ladies were so nice and comforting to me. Traci asked me if I was ready to put my dress on. She said, "Your fiancé' and I picked this out for you. He emailed me a picture, and I just picked up some styles and let him have the final choice. He did a splendid job."

This dress was all lace and form fitting. The dress came off of the shoulders and the lace imprints laid on my skin like a beautiful design. He did not choose any shoes, though. I wore a beautiful strand of pearls and pearl studs. She looked at me after I was dressed and said, "You look just as I imagined."

Angie was very emotional. She said, "I don't know you, but I am so happy for you. Our company is so thankful to have been chosen to plan your special day. Traci, it's time! Charity, come meet your groom."

They walked me to a runway of rose petals, and from out of nowhere, Ralph came and intertwined his arms with mine. While I was looking at him trying not to cry, Corrine walked out with her little basket of rose petals. Oh my goodness, they both looked amazing. The music started, and it was one of my favorite songs by The Temptations, "This is My Promise." Ivan sang this song with backup and a saxophone player.

This is my dream wedding. There were so many people there. As the tears cleared and I could make out faces, it was Ivan's family and my mother! I love this man! The wedding was beautiful, and the weather was perfect. The reception was on the beach, and as the sun was setting, we danced in a stream of its beauty. Finally, I know love, I am loved, I love myself, and my kids will see and live with true love and leadership in the home.

There was no sexual addiction; there was loneliness that needed to be filled no matter the cost to my spirit, body or soul. For as much damage as I felt, I am blessed to experience the polar opposite in love and gratitude. Amen!

My Healing from Secret Pain

Pain

My Truth

A doctor can give you instructions on how to relieve pain from broken bones, toothaches, and various surgeries. It's up to you to take their advice on how to keep down the amount of pain you suffer during those times. Even the doctor will give you medicine to help you numb the pain, just so you don't have to feel or think. You can escape in a pill-induced sleep only to wake up feeling a little better than you did before laying down. The bottle says in four hours take another pill so you can numb your pain again.

When you are trying to heal from secret pain and heartache, it is impossible for one person to tell anyone how to heal. We all handle our things differently for our personality types. Some of us use the following to numb the anguish of deep pain: food, alcohol, drugs, sex, religion, prescription pills, blaming others, blaming God or we simply become an angry, bitter person. Everyone has a different voice for dealing with their stuff. I can only share my personal healing with you and yet I am still healing as I write this book.

Being raped, violated me mentally and physically and parts of my soul died at a very early age. To recover physically is a matter of time. The mental memories of the rape are what I've struggled with throughout my adult life.

When we are children, one of our first group of things to learn are our five senses; hear, touch, smell, taste and seeing. Here is my breakdown: I can still hear the sound of his voice as he yelled for me to hold him tighter and scratch his back so that he could feel as good as I did. Really, dude! I remember touching my leg and feeling the moisture run down and the tears streaming down my face like a river that has no ending. The pain from my head as my hair was used to drag me up the stairs. The smell in the room was damp and cold even though it was hot outside. The cologne that he wore. Thirty-three years later if I smell it, my heart races and my eyes survey the room to see if he is in my presence.

When I was thirty years old, I was in a store, and I smelled that cologne. I froze in my tracks in the middle of the bread aisle and started screaming for my seven -year-old daughter like a crazy person. She came running to me. I grabbed her hand, swiftly walked to the car, locked all the doors and sat there with both hands glued to the steering wheel with the windows up in June. I came to myself when I felt her hand on my shoulder as she said, "Mom, what's wrong? I responded,"Nothing,honey." Oh, I'm sure she believed me as I was checking to make sure I had not pulled her arm out of place. All I could think about was if he touched my child, we would tear up that bread aisle, and he would lose.

The sight of the walls of the room and the missing light bulb that I focused on while my body was being pushed back and forth with every thrust from his body. The taste of blood in my mouth from biting the inside of my lip and the unusual taste of his tongue as it was forced into my mouth. He ripped my virginity from me when I wanted to stay a virgin until I got married. Destroyed my thoughts about what a relationship was because I was his choice yet he was not mine. I can't find one part of this event that felt good for me!

So, does that make him a monster to violate me and want me to like it? In that time, I would have said, yes. As mercy has set in during my process of healing, I see an insecure man that was incapable of creating a relationship with a consenting adult. Therefore, he chose to force a child that looked grown, to be his woman. Insecurity is the culprit.

As a rape victim, I felt as though I could have done something different or wore something less revealing. What if I had not been in the right place at the wrong time; maybe if I had not been so trusting. All of these would have, could have or should haves can't take the place of the word no, but that word meant absolutely nothing. The tears that streamed from my eyes and hit that mattress during my attack were tears of innocence, guilt, shame and loss of self-love.

Healing from rape is something that takes as long as it takes. But one thing I have acknowledged is that it happened, yes I was damaged, yes I was told that I would not ever have children due to the damage that was done to my body.

My healing began when I got married on Christmas Day of 1989 and had my son on September 30, 1990. Then on November 19, 1991 my baby girl was born. He did not win! God won, and He makes the decisions, not man. My children saved my life and built my faith.

Some people live in their pain from the hidden acts done to them in their youth for the rest of their lives because there is no one there to pour words of love and light into their lives. But when you think about it, if it is a secret how can someone else help heal you if they don't know that you are suffering. For some, they have told the story and the family took up for the predator because it was a brother, uncle or cousin. The next violation comes when that victim is told not to tell and to grow up because things happen. No matter what, share your story! Maybe it is a story of a broken heart from a marriage of lies or the loneliness of longing for a love of your own. Maybe it's from the very silence in the room of life, and there is no light within you to be noticed. I promise there is someone that is experiencing your pain on a lower or higher level.

For me, healing comes from being an excellent storyteller. If I can share one thing in my life that makes me a relatable source for another person, my job is done.

My silence is broken, and my healing is on a path. With each story, another person joins me on this journey from the depths of the silent screams on to the journey of healing from our secret pain.

In Closing

We all have a story. Whether it is good or bad, it is your story. If you have silent screams that you have been holding quietly within, and they are holding you back from being whole and living a full life from the inside out; I want to encourage you to write it down and free yourself. Just remember, that we don't go through life's ups and downs just for us. We go through so that we can experience the process and tell about the victory on the other side of the Silent Screams.

More about LJ

LJ is the Author of The Master Relationship Builder –Relationship Building through the Eyes of the Employee. A good workplace culture is vital to the growth of a sound company. Leaders should treat each employee as if they are a part of the vision of the company. LJ is available to assist leaders and employees on the necessity of building a fertile environment for growth as a team.

LJ is also available for any group or organization that would like a speaker for overcoming the silent screams.

Contact:
LJ Crawford
PO Box 1483
Hixson, TN 37343
LJCtheauthor@gmail.com
LJCMOTIVATIONS.com

www.ingramcontent.com/pod-product-compliance
Lightning Source LLC
Chambersburg PA
CBHW070106280626
47159CB00016B/1468